I0596606

THE GIFT OF TYLER

THE GIFT OF THE ELEMENTS SERIES

BY C.S. ELSTON

SHINE-A-LIGHT
PRESS

Visit Shine-A-Light Press on our website:
    www.ShineALightPress.com
    on Twitter: @SALPress
    And on Facebook: www.facebook.com/SALPress

Visit The Gift of Tyler on our website:
    www.GiftOfTheElements.com
    on Twitter: @GiftOfTheElements
    And on Facebook: www.facebook.com/GiftOfTheElements

Visit C.S. Elston on his website:
    www.cselston.com
    on Twitter: @cselston
    And on Facebook: www.facebook.com/cselston

The Shine-A-Light Press logo is a trademark of Shine-A-Light Corp.

Publisher's Note: *The Gift of Tyler* is a work of fiction. Where real people, events, establishments, organizations, or locales appear, they are used fictitiously. All other elements of the novel are drawn from the author's imagination and any resemblance to actual persons or events is coincidental.

Scripture quotations are taken from *The Holy Bible, New International Version,* Copyright © 1973, 1978, 1984 by International Bible Society.

Author's Photo by Christie Bruno

ISBN 978-0-997-67220-6

Library of Congress Control Number: 2016937289

Printed in the U.S.A.

For my parents, whom I was still living with when I first conceived this story nearly two decades before it saw the light of day and who have gone way above and beyond the call of duty to support me and my crazy dreams.

Acknowledgments

As always, I would like to extend my deepest gratitude to my original proofreaders: My parents, Doug and Judy; my father-in-law, Craig; my sister, Jennifer; and my wife, Andrea. They have all been supportive in numerous ways, not the least of which is having read drafts of the book before publication and offering valuable feedback.

Table of Contents

THE GIFT OF TYLER

THE GIFT OF THE ELEMENTS SERIES

BY C.S. ELSTON

...the Lord God formed the man from the dust of the ground and breathed into his nostrils the breath of life, and the man became a living being.

- Genesis 2:7

CHAPTER ONE
Trippin' In 1972

1972 was the longest year in history. No, this is not an attack on Richard Nixon or a commentary on either the Winter Olympics in Sapporo, Japan or the Christmas bombing of North Vietnam. Within the context of Coordinated Universal Time, 1972 was literally the longest year ever. Two seconds were added during the 366-day leap year in order to keep the time of day close to the mean solar time. A single second is occasionally added but the two extra seconds added on a leap year officially made 1972 the longest year in history. That, however, was not the most significant thing about 1972.

Whereas some might celebrate the births of celebrities like Shaquille O'Neal and Ben Affleck which occurred that year, and some might mourn the deaths of notables like King Edward VIII and Harry Truman in 1972, something even more amazing happened that year. It happened four times in four different locations around the world. Each event had only two witnesses: a messenger, and a recipient. No one else was aware of these extraordinary happenings at the time because their impact would not be revealed to the rest of the world for another twenty-five years, and they would be shown in spectacular ways.

The recipient of the message in Seattle, Washington was a sweet, pretty, Caucasian seventeen year-old girl with long brunette hair flowing down her back. Just before it happened, Flower Hirsch, as was her normal routine, was walking west down the North Seattle sidewalk of Roosevelt Way in her pink waitress uniform, having just ended her dinner-rush shift at Eddie's Diner. She lamented the smell of cooking grease and potatoes that penetrated her nostrils with every gust of wind that brushed over her dress or breezed through her hair. She couldn't wait to get out of those clothes and into the shower every time she left the diner. This night was no exception.

As usual, she turned left to enter her parents' driveway. Then she walked the same old sixteen steps uphill toward the white single-car garage door that was outlined by sky blue-painted trim. She turned right onto the concrete path below the living room window, which was framed in bricks. Bricks covered about three quarters of the front of the house if you didn't count the garage door. The rest of the house consisted of windows that were set into either white frames or frames painted with that same sky blue color that surrounded the garage door.

She walked eleven paces along the path that was flanked on both sides by eight-inch flowerbeds and ultimately stepped onto the small, concrete, rod iron-framed porch in front of the main entrance. She knew that the next step was to enter the 1,402 square foot rambler shaped like a shoe-box. However, home was not a place she had a strong desire to be. It never really had been but that feeling had grown stronger in recent months and tonight it seemed to be peaking.

This was Saturday night and her parents were throwing one of their typical parties. Flower could make out every note of Iron Butterfly's *In-A-Gadda-Da-Vida* as it blared from inside. The only thing stronger than the sound of the music was the smell of the marijuana emanating from the same open windows.

She paused on the porch to sigh deeply at the thought of entering a house inhabited by her thirty-five year-old parents and their friends, all of whom had lived every moment of the hippie-era to its fullest and showed no signs of giving it up any time soon. Trying to swallow her desire to escape this home and, with her exhale now complete and the draw of the shower pulling her inside, she reached forward and gripped the cold metal handle on the screen door.

She paused again, feeling like an ex-convict choosing to go

back to prison without having committed a single crime. Guilt set in for a moment. Her home environment wasn't horrible. Her parents were really nice people. She was just tired of being the youngest person in the house and yet, somehow, also feeling like the only adult, especially since she was the only one in the family who technically wasn't an adult yet. She sighed a second time as she pressed her thumb in on the button that unlocked the screen door and slowly swung it open. Taking a third and final deep breath, she stepped in front of the door and let it hit her in the backside, practically unnoticed, as she exhaled and reached for the doorknob on the front door to complete the seemingly excruciating process.

"Flower," a voice called out calmly from behind her. Startled, she spun around to find an elderly woman standing in the driveway who had not been there just seconds ago.

"Oh," Flower exclaimed with her heart suddenly racing. "Oh, my… You… You scared…" Flower studied the woman's straight hair that hung below her waistline in the back and hippie-style clothing, complete with a tie-dyed caftan, and concluded that this must be one of her parents' friends tripping the light fantastic. "Can I help you? Are you a friend of my parents?"

"Should I call you Flower?" The woman inquired. "I'm assuming it's too soon to call you Kathleen."

"Excuse me?" Flower exclaimed with shocked confusion.

"How could you possibly know…?" She hadn't told anyone of her secret plan to change her name so, how could this woman know what she had just revealed? That was absolutely impossible. Thoughts of a hallucinogenic drug opening the woman's mind and transforming her into some kind of psychic flashed through Flower's brain, even though she knew that wasn't really possible. Her thoughts were interrupted by the woman who began speaking again.

"You're changing your name next week," the woman stated matter-of-factly. "After you turn eighteen, I mean. You just haven't told them yet." She pointed to the house, clearly referring to Flower's parents, before continuing. "You haven't even told them you're moving out."

Growing more perplexed by the second, Flower started to get angry. She didn't even notice that *In-A-Gadda-Da-Vida* had ended and someone was playing *Fortunate Son* by Creedence Clearwater Revival in the background. "You might be high as a kite but I know I'm not. So, start explaining yourself. Are you going to tell me who you are and how you know what you think you know? Or, am I going to have to call the police?"

"I'm no one of great consequence, Flower. Just a humble messenger."

"The police it is then," Flower said as she turned and reached for the front door. But, once again, she was stopped by the woman's voice.

"You'll have a son one day. He'll be exactly your age when you realize how special he is. You will come to realize that he's not just a gift to you, but to everyone."

"You're crazy," Flower stated as she spun around and discovered that the woman was already gone. She stared in silence for a moment before finally admitting, "That, or, maybe I am."

Flower continued to stand, staring in silence for a few additional moments, wondering if she was the one tripping the light fantastic. Was the marijuana in the air laced with something that she had inhaled secondhand causing her to hallucinate what she had just experienced? It would be decades before she found her answer. But, the answer would most definitely come. And, although it wouldn't involve any narcotics, it would be absolutely mind blowing.

1997 & Everything In Between

To the casual observer, the first several months of 1997 made it appear to be about as normal as any year could be. Of course there were notable deaths, like East Coast rapper The Notorious B.I.G. and NASCAR driver John Nemechek, but every year has that to some extent. 1997 was shaping up to be, by most counts, as common as the Wednesday on which it began. However, 1997 was the year that events prophesied in 1972 to four different people in four different locations around the world, including a young Seattle girl named Flower, would finally happen.

But, for Flower, the events that transpired in the two and a half decades between the prophecy and its fulfillment are what made it all possible. Just as the elderly woman who appeared to Flower in her parents' driveway had predicted, Flower changed her name to Kathleen on her eighteenth birthday. Almost immediately afterward, she spent over half the money she'd saved working at Eddie's Diner on a blue and yellow 1959 Wartburg 311. She drove home, told her parents she was fed up with being the most mature person in the house and packed her new car with all of her belongings. The fully-loaded car looked like the camping limousine the previous owner had told her it was advertised to be when it was new. She pulled out of the driveway with a mixed sense of fear and relief and headed out to find what she considered a "normal" life.

To her surprise and true to the stereotypical hippie attitude, her parents had said that they thought it was "far out" she was finally showing some free spirit by heading out on her own to find herself. It wasn't exactly the start to her journey that she expected, being far from a normal parental send-off, but she chalked it up as par for the course and hit the road to close that chapter of her life and start a new one.

Her journey ended only three hours from where it began but that was enough. Away, even if it wasn't far away, was still away.

She had stopped for lunch, and only lunch, in a small town called Penuel in the middle of Eastern Washington State. Kathleen stepped out of the car and gave her body a half-hearted stretch as she looked up and down Main Street. It was an old-fashioned, quaint farming town with little activity. She immediately spotted an antique shop and a general store, but no sign of any customers. As she turned 360 degrees, the only places she saw with any customers at all were a gas station about a block away and a butcher shop two doors down. Each place had just had one customer. *Not exactly a booming metropolis*, she thought to herself.

She peeked into the window of the diner she had parked in front of. Other than the fact that there were only four customers, it was not so different from the one she had just quit working in. She opened the door, strolled inside, and took a whiff of the familiar bacon scent left over from breakfast. Fearing there were no better options in town, she sat down and ordered a turkey sandwich without even looking at the menu.

It wasn't very busy, considering that it was the lunch hour, so she and the middle-aged waitress, Gwen, talked quite a bit. Kathleen hadn't noticed the *Help Wanted* sign on the way in but Gwen was quick to point it out when she learned of Kathleen's work experience.

Kathleen gave it some thought while she ate. She knew the money she had left would quickly run out if she didn't start bringing some more in right away. Plus, as she looked around the diner, she knew this slower paced environment, while not the big change she was looking for, would be better than the one she had just left.

When she finally agreed to stay and take the job, it was supposed to be temporary. But, for Kathleen, time passed quickly and that offer ultimately evolved into a new home, a new best friend and mother figure, and employment that lasted eight years until 1980 when her newly established world was turned upside down.

Gwen had a heart attack and died right there behind the diner's counter during the breakfast shift. The diner closed for six months until a man named Val Stafford re-opened it without Kathleen's help.

By then, she had taken a job as a teller at the local bank. She had also briefly let a man named Brett Riggle "wriggle" his way into her life when she was weak from grief over Gwen's passing. He didn't treat her well and the relationship was never meant to last. "Emotionally abusive" is what psychiatrists typically call it – not that Kathleen could ever afford a psychiatrist.

Kathleen was saved from the experience of having to break things off with him though because he vanished immediately upon hearing the word "pregnant." Brett's exit was a welcome one and the start of yet another chapter in her life. She indefinitely gave up dating altogether but finally decided after eight years that Penuel was her permanent home. It would be tougher without Gwen but easier without Brett and baby Tyler's arrival was the best thing that had ever happened to Kathleen.

She, of course, had fears that stemmed from being left alone with the responsibility of raising this innocent child. But, his presence also, somehow, gave her comfort. Even the birthing process had been smoother than Kathleen had anticipated. There was severe pain and Tyler came out crying like all babies do. But, the whole thing only took a couple of hours and even Tyler's crying stopped about seven or eight minutes after that. Tyler simply made Kathleen's life better from the start and she knew that he would be her focus and her joy from that point on.

She made banking her career largely because it gave her consistent hours, which were never something she could count on when she was working as a waitress. Once Tyler was born, those consistent hours became vital to her existence. She had to call in favors and trade pies and meals to make sure Tyler was always cared for while she was at work. She even occasionally had to shell out a little cash for a babysitter but it was always worth it. There was nothing she looked forward to more than her time with Tyler.

A lot of moms have favorite phases of their children's upbringing but Kathleen truly felt that each was somehow even better than the last. Probably because Tyler was such a great kid. He was never the smartest or the most athletic. Tyler was just flat out good. He made the right decisions from an early age both at home and at school. Tyler also challenged her in good ways and managed to get her to look at things from other points of view.

From the beginning, Tyler was a gift. And, just as the woman in her parents' driveway had predicted twenty-five years earlier, 1997 was the year she would discover that he wasn't just a gift to her, but to the whole world.

CHAPTER THREE
Tyler

Tyler was twisted up like an Auntie Anne's soft pretzel as he slept soundly and peacefully in his bed. The song "The Good Life" by the Los Angeles based rock band Weezer was playing from his radio alarm and was doing less to wake him up and more to provide the soundtrack to a fantastic dream. His childhood friend Jessie, who had since become one of the most popular girls in school, was suddenly confessing her eternal, undying, and profoundly immeasurable love for him. Tyler wasn't a morning person but, even more than usual, if he had been aware that this was only a dream, he wouldn't ever have wanted to wake up.

His room was fairly typical for an American teenager in the nineteen-nineties. However, unlike certain peers of his, the posters that lined Tyler's walls were not that of exotic sports cars, athletes or bikini-clad women. His walls were covered in meticulously chosen posters of his very favorite modern rock 'n' rollers.

The nineties were a great time for a teenager to be from Washington State. The whole country had gone crazy for "The Seattle Sound" and, therefore, most teenagers in Washington loved to claim Seattle as their own – even if it was hundreds of miles away.

"Grunge music," which took its inspirations from hardcore punk and heavy metal, was characterized by heavily distorted electric guitars and growling vocals that accentuated the angst-filled lyrics of the songs the bands played. It began to emerge in the mid-eighties and was popularized in the early nineties by two primary bands: Mother Love Bone and Nirvana.

Mother Love Bone formed in 1988 but their promising career ended in 1990 when lead singer Andrew Wood died of a heroin overdose. However, the members of the band split up, found two new singers, and formed two new bands: Soundgarden and Pearl Jam.

Nirvana released their first album in 1989 but subsequently left the local music label Sub Pop and signed with major label DGC Records. They released *Nevermind* just a month after Pearl Jam released their immensely popular album *Ten* and only a couple of weeks before Soundgarden released *Badmotorfinger*. The Fall of 1991 was the beginning of the Grunge explosion into pop culture.

What followed was a wave of bands that pulled from the same sound. Alice in Chains released *Dirt*, Stone Temple Pilots released *Core* and the underground sound began to hit the mainstream. By the end of the nineties, most of the bands were gone but the influence of the Seattle sound would permeate rock music for decades.

Tyler's walls showed signs of that Seattle sound with posters of grunge bands like the originals: Nirvana, Pearl Jam, and Soundgarden; as well as later arrivals like Alice In Chains and The Smashing Pumpkins. But, it also showed the signs of a changing tide with posters of bands like Radiohead, Bush, Oasis and Silverchair who were all from places much further away.

Additionally typical of an American teenager, clothes were strewn all over the room which was also full of the nineties versions of computer stuff, video game accessories, and school books. There were also a few remnants of night snacking such as dirty dishes, half-empty bottles of soda, and completely empty bags of chips that hadn't yet been cleaned up.

A knock on the door and the sound of his mom's voice woke Tyler up, but to call his initial state as being one of "consciousness" might be a stretch.

"Tyler," Kathleen called apprehensively from the other side of his door. "Hurry up or you'll be late for school again."

"That's the idea," Tyler responded as his eyes remained

closed but his hand began searching for his alarm button. "Sleep is so much better than school."

"I'm sure there are very few people who would argue with you about that," Kathleen admitted. "But, don't you still have to show up on time?"

Ultimately, his hand finally hit a shoe on his nightstand and the alarm turned off. As tired as he was, he didn't even realize he never touched his alarm and therefore had no idea that something extraordinary had just taken place.

"Nah," Tyler teased. "But thanks for asking."

"I'm serious," Kathleen fired back. "The question was rhetorical. I'm not really asking, Tyler. Get up. Now."

Tyler sat up but still didn't open his eyes as he responded, "I'm up! Geez! We can't all be full of sunshine in the morning."

"Do I need to direct you to the sunshine out your window and the fact that it means you need to move that lazy butt of yours?"

"I'm not lazy! You're just interrupting a really good dream…"

"Will telling me about it help you wake up?"

After a brief pause in which Tyler faced the reality of admitting his feelings for Jesse which no one but he considered a secret, "I already said I'm up! Let me get ready in peace, will ya?"

"Fine. But, I need to hear movement in there," Kathleen told him with not-so-subtle skepticism infused into her voice.

Ready to put on a show, Tyler laid back down. He repeatedly kicked and punched his bed like a toddler pitching a hissy fit before asking, "How's that?"

"A good start. Move it, or lose it, kid."

"I'm moving! Holy cow…"

Vigorously rubbing the sleep out of his eyes and opening them wide in an overstated expanse meant to speed up the process of adjusting from dark to light, Tyler yawned and stretched his way to a standing position with absolutely no enthusiasm whatsoever. He was an appealing looking kid but not the traditionally popular type. Although he was well liked, with no athletic affiliations or anything equivalent, he was living a conventional middle-of-the-road high school existence. All in all, it was a perfectly adequate way to go. Things could have been much worse. But, it wasn't exactly ideal either. Certainly, there were things in his life he would change if he could. If he had his druthers, he would probably start by making the dream from which he had just been so rudely interrupted, a reality.

Tyler looked around the room as his eyes gained focus and started putting his school books in his backpack. He searched the disaster area for clean clothes and, after rounding up some jeans and a hoodie, opened the door and stepped out into the hallway to head for the bathroom.

After his "morning relief" session, Tyler stood in front of the sink and gave himself a "hobo shower" to save time. He leaned down and got his hair wet before throwing gel into it and re-styling it, used a washcloth and soap to clean his armpits before re-deodorizing, and finished up by brushing his teeth.

He put his clean clothes on before returning to his room for his backpack, shoes and socks. He decided to throw a plaid shirt on over his hoodie and, short of having breakfast, could then consider himself ready for the day.

However, there was no way for Tyler to truly be ready because he couldn't possibly know how this day would absolutely change everything he had ever known about his entire existence. The shoe alarm incident that had completely escaped his notice would have been a preview of what was to come on the same scale as a two second movie trailer would be for a three and a half hour epic adventure. In other words, the snowflake that had just fallen would soon be rolling itself into a mountain-sized snowball.

CHAPTER FOUR
Breakfast Tsunami

Kathleen had grown into a conservative-looking but very attractive forty-two year-old woman. Her hair was still long but not as long as it had been when she was a seventeen year-old girl. Her hair had more body now and she dressed and did her make up in a manner specifically designed to present a professional appearance. It was a notch above the effort put out by the other employees of the small town bank and may have been a subconscious way of holding on to a piece of the big city she had left behind twenty-five years earlier.

She didn't have to be at the bank for over an hour so, she found herself scrambling eggs in a metal frying pan on the stovetop. She used a wooden spoon so she didn't scratch the non-stick surface but her lifting and folding movement had slowed down considerably in the last couple of minutes. Her focus was now divided between stirring the eggs and the small, muted television set on the kitchen counter displaying a "breaking news story" about a tsunami off the coast of Japan.

The old familiar smell of the diners she used to work in filled the air but it no longer bothered her like it once did. In fact, with her attention already divided this morning, the smell was barely registering in her brain and certainly wasn't bringing up any nostalgia.

Tyler tottered into the kitchen and sat down in front of the table where he already had a place setting waiting for him, along with a carton of orange juice, a piece of toast and several slices of applewood smoked bacon. This was all part of the routine the two of them had established a long time ago.

"Good morning sleepy head," Kathleen teased as she snapped out of her trance, spun around and slid some eggs onto his plate. She followed the action up by sliding the remainder of the scrambled eggs onto her own plate at the place setting next to his.

"What's going on?" Tyler asked as he finished pouring his orange juice and set the carton down, pointing to the television with his other hand.

"Oh, a huge tsunami off the coast of Japan. They're calling it a miracle."

"What?" Tyler inquired. "How could a disaster be a miracle?"

"There was virtually no disaster," Kathleen declared. "That's the whole point."

"Okay," Tyler said hesitantly as he tried to wade through the waves of confusion. "Whenever you're ready, you can now start making sense."

"No…"

"No? Meaning, you have no intention of making sense?"

"Let me finish," Kathleen fought back. "The waves were heading right for Tokyo and they never made it past the shoreline. They're estimating that the number of lives saved could be as many as a hundred thousand."

Still confused, Tyler continued pressing. "How did the waves not go beyond the shoreline?"

"No one knows," Kathleen persisted. "But, some people are claiming to have seen a teenaged girl on the beach with her arms stretched out and they say it looked like she was actually holding the waves back."

"What?"

"Seriously. Then the wall of water crashed down and took her out to sea. So, the death toll dropped from a hundred thousand to one."

"Get out of here."

"I will not. This is my kitchen and I'm just telling you what they said," Kathleen insisted before noticing something was missing from her son's face. "Hey, you're not wearing your glasses."

"I'm not?"

"Don't be a smart alec."

"I guess I forgot," Tyler supposed with sincere bewilderment.

"Stop it. I told you, you'd look better in those contacts I bought you."

Finally taking a bite of his scrambled eggs, Tyler confessed. "I'm not wearing any contacts either."

"What do you mean?" Kathleen asked as she stood behind her chair and set her butter and jam smothered toast down on her plate after taking a bite out of it.

"I mean there are no vision enhancing devices on my eyes of any kind."

"Then why aren't you squinting?"

"I don't know. But, I can see just fine."

"I guess we have a miracle of our own brewing right here, huh?"

"Yeah, I guess so…"

Staring at her son without expression, Kathleen finally smacked him playfully on the shoulder and exclaimed, "Stop it. That's impossible, Tyler."

"Obviously not. Weird though, huh?"

"Eyes don't get better," Kathleen maintained while sitting down and leaning forward to study Tyler's eyes. "They get worse.

Trust me. I go in every year and walk out with a new prescription."

"I'm aware of the norm on this subject, mom. I've been having the same experience for about five years now, myself."

"You have to be wearing contacts."

"Mom," Tyler said in frustration. "I told you, I'm not."

"Yes, you are. You have to be. You just don't want to admit I was right."

"Right about what?" Tyler questioned.

"About how much better you look without your glasses on."

Tyler was tired of putting up the fight so he finally caved in and told a little white lie, mostly to put his mom's mind at ease. "Alright fine. I'm wearing contacts."

"I knew it. You can barely even see them. Nice. You really do look good."

"Thanks," Tyler said as he let the subject go and looked back at the TV set on the counter. He allowed his mind to wander, contemplating both what had just happened to him and what he was seeing played out on the television. He couldn't help but think about the possibility of miracles. This wasn't something he had previously given a lot of thought to. He certainly believed in God so, he felt like he had to believe miracles were possible. But, he had never witnessed one himself and wasn't sure they still happened.

However, something he had once read by C.S. Lewis popped into his mind. He wasn't even sure where he'd read it. Only that he had. The C.S. Lewis books he actually remembered reading back when he was a kid were the Chronicles of Narnia series. Those were about witches, fauns and talking beavers, which would be a miracle Tyler wouldn't mind witnessing. But, the statement that he was remembering, he didn't believe had come from any of those books. C.S. Lewis, somewhere, had written something about the fact that the extraordinary cannot be recognized until you have first discovered what is ordinary. That belief in miracles did not depend on an ignorance of the laws of nature. On the contrary, it is only possible to the extent that those laws are known. Or, at least, he believed it was something close to that. That was, the general idea anyway.

Tyler thought about it for a moment or two while he nibbled on his deliciously salty bacon. Perhaps the impossible was only impossible because no one had yet discovered that it was actually possible. If that were true, would that make everything possible? And, if everything was possible, would nothing be a miracle? Or, would everything be a miracle? *This philosophical hooey is way too deep for breakfast*, he ultimately decided as he finally let go of his unexplainable eyesight improvement and brushed off the tsunami incident as false hearsay with no clue as to how much stranger this day would soon become.

CHAPTER FIVE
High School

With Tyler behind the wheel, a red 1988 Chevrolet Cheyenne pickup truck rolled into the high school parking lot and into a parking space in the second row of vehicles all belonging to students. This parking lot was located on the South side of the building that contained the school's offices while the staff parking lot, which was much smaller, was located around the corner on the East side of the same building.

Tyler's truck was something he truly appreciated. In part, he appreciated it because it symbolized his independence and freedom as well as a stepping-stone into adulthood. But, even more so, his appreciation came from the way in which he had obtained the truck. About six months before his sixteenth birthday, his mom had informed Tyler that she would come up with the money to pay for half of whatever vehicle he decided he wanted. That meant that Tyler had to come up with the other half. So, he started taking whatever odd jobs a fifteen year-old boy could find. He mowed lawns, painted fences and even milked some cows. When he turned sixteen, he hadn't saved enough to be satisfied. So, he kept working and about eight months later he had saved almost $3,400. Kathleen was so impressed that she rounded up so he had an even $7,000 to go shopping with. Mr. Roberge, the farmer for whom Tyler had milked the cows, cut his price on the truck he was selling by $999 because he recognized that Tyler was a good kid. He had been driving the red Cheyenne ever since.

Only seconds behind Tyler and his truck was his best friend, Preston, an unusual eighteen year-old who could be an attractive young man if he stopped trying so hard to keep up with trends while simultaneously putting far too much effort into being unique. Travelling at a velocity just beyond the line that caps any reasonable safety standards, Preston drove into the adjacent parking space on Tyler's left-hand side and came to an abrupt stop with a brief screech of the tires. He looked over at Tyler for approval and caught his friend's eye line.

Tyler gave Preston a wave with his right hand without any acknowledgment of the obnoxious driving maneuvers. He reached for the door handle with his left hand, not noticing that the handle had positioned itself into his hand completely on its own. Unaware that the phenomena were continuing to happen wherever he went that morning, Tyler stepped out of his truck and grabbed his backpack from the uncovered bed.

Like the bottom of a teenager's skateboard, Preston's light blue 1982 Renault Fuego was plastered with every lame bumper sticker imaginable from *I Love It When They Call Me Big Papa* to *Fat People Are Harder To Kidnap*. Preston leapt out of his clunky beater of a car in his wide-leg carpenter pants that sagged off his backside, a Tommy Hilfiger American flag sweatshirt, a crooked Seattle SuperSonics baseball cap, and fake Buddy Holly frames with no glass in them. He had nothing to carry and immediately greeted Tyler with merriment. "Good morning, sweetheart."

"Hey," Tyler responded.

"Sleep well?"

"Once you finally let me hang up the phone around three o'clock in the morning, yeah, I did. Thanks."

"Come on," Preston taunted. "You love it. If I didn't shower you with so much attention, who would? Huh?"

"My mom," Tyler deadpanned as he put his arms through his backpack straps.

"But I'm better at it."

"Debatable."

"Ouch. That really hurts. I've got her in the looks department though, right?"

"Absolutely not."

"Ow! You're killin' me here, man. Give me something. Am I at least more entertaining?"

"Yeah," Tyler conceded. "I think you have her on that one."

"Finally. This lady's packin' some mad skills. She's harder to bring down than a nun's skirt."

"Easy," Tyler responded. "You're crossing a couple of lines there."

"What lines?"

"That's bordering on sacrilegious and you're talking about my mom."

"It's a compliment to both. The nun is being faithful to her sacred vow and your mom is an amazing woman."

"Okay. Good call. And, you're right, you are more entertaining."

"Of course I'm right. I'm always right. I'm a freaking Albert Einstein meets Sigmund Freud genius over here. I've got it all balled up into one big Preston."

"You're one big somethin' alright," Tyler said as he chuckled to himself and nodded his head toward Preston's car. "How's she holdin' up?"

"My hooptie?"

"Your car."

"My hooptie," Preston agreed. "She's good. It's like a long, healthy marriage."

"You've barely had her two years."

"Exactly. I see the younger hotter models but I'm not even considering trading her in because she already knows how I like to ride."

"Again you've barely had her two years," Tyler told his friend as he continued to chuckle.

"That's twice as long you've had your truck, hombre. You should be coming to me for marriage advice."

"Fair enough," Tyler conceded. "Hombre, huh?"

"That's right."

"You know, I might like you more if you were Mexican."

"You love me because I'm like the United Nations. Best of all cultures. All worlds."

"Best, or worst?" Tyler asked, jokingly, while he dropped his head and looked down at the pavement.

"That's cold, man." Preston feigned emotional scarring with a dramatic flair.

"You know I'm kidding," Tyler reassured him half-heartedly, knowing they were both in on the joke, as he kicked a small rock. He quickly looked up again without realizing that the rock he'd kicked rolled through the parking lot, hopped a curb and flower bed, then bounced across the street and disappeared in the field on the other side of it. Instead, Tyler spotted a cocky jock named Graham pulling into the parking lot in his flashy black 1995

Chevrolet Camaro Z-28. Tyler despised Graham but, to make matters worse, in the passenger seat was his Jessie, the girl he'd been in love with for nearly a decade. She was a beautiful, smart, sweet eighteen year-old girl who broke his heart every single day. Seeing her with Graham now was a painful reminder that the dream he was having when he woke up this morning was exactly that: a dream. But, it was a really good dream. It included every component he needed in a dream to place it in the upper echelon of dreams. Of course, the list of components was a short one. Jessie was actually the only item on it. He briefly wished he could go home, crawl back into bed, and re-enter that dream. The only problem with that, if it were possible, is that he would want to live in that dream forever.

"Hey," Preston started, "dig the contacts."

Distracted, Tyler watched as Graham parked just a few cars away. As Jessie was getting out of the passenger side of the car, Tyler was probably the only one who took note of the fact that she had an unusually urban upscale look for a teenager in a small farming town. She was gorgeous. Of course he noticed.

Graham suddenly reached over and pulled her back inside of the Camaro to kiss her. It wasn't even eight o'clock in the morning yet and she'd already broken Tyler's heart again. "Yeah," Tyler finally responded to Preston, "thanks."

"You're so pretty," Preston mocked. Trying to figure out

what was distracting Tyler, he started to ask, "What are you staring…" But, he quickly caught on and continued, "Oh. Don't worry about those two, mate."

"Mate?" Tyler finally snapped out of his trance. "What are you Australian all of a sudden?"

"What's wrong with mate?"

"Nothing. If you're Australian."

"United Nations. Come on," Preston proposed as he tried to change the subject. "Let's get inside before Graham decides to chamois his car with our faces."

The subject change was successful and into the high school they went.

"You hear about that tsunami in Japan?" Tyler asked.

"Yeah," Preston concurred. "Whack, right?"

"Doesn't get much weirder than that."

And yet, it would soon get much, much stranger.

CHAPTER SIX
Earth Science

Mr. Russell, a porky man in his sixties, sported a bald head surrounded by salt and pepper hair wrapped around the sides and back like a horseshoe. Cementing the nerd-vibe, he accented his face with thick horn-rimmed glasses and a mustache that would make Tom Selleck jealous.

On this day, as was true approximately one hundred and eighty days out of the calendar year, Mr. Russell lectured at the front of a fairly typical nineteen-nineties high school science classroom. The room was complete with standard epoxy resin counter tops and polyolefin sinks instead of the desks that one would find in other types of classrooms. To complete the scientific learning experience the students, of course, sat on stools instead of in chairs. The key physical clues as to the subject of the lesson on that particular day were the three rocks resting on the counter top in front of each individual student.

"There are three different great classes of rocks," Mr. Russell instructed. "Each class is represented by the three rocks you have in front of you. On your left, you have a sedimentary rock. In the middle, is an igneous rock. And, finally, on the right, is a metamorphic rock."

While most of the students stared down at their rocks, either interested in what Mr. Russell was teaching or pretending to be, Tyler and Preston sat in the back of the room talking to each other. They were paying little attention to anything but their own conversation and no attention at all to Mr. Russell.

"Did you see the shirt Virginia Leigh is wearing today?" Preston asked while holding his hands out in front of him to make the international sign for big boobs. "Boom! Yeah, she was out sick last week. Right. Doctor's appointment for sure. Not a general practitioner though. Quite an improvement I have to say, too. Like an upgraded Ginger Spice. I'll tell you what I want – what I really, really want. Yes, Virgina. That was totally worth the wait. Am I right?"

Mr. Russell had stopped lecturing to watch Preston. Just before Tyler could inquire as to exactly who it was that Preston thought had been waiting for Virginia Leigh's operation, Mr. Russell made an inquiry of his own. "Is there something you want to share with the class, Preston?"

Had Virginia been in the classroom, Preston probably

would have considered her feelings enough to keep his mouth shut. However, Virginia wasn't present. So, without hesitating, Preston responded, "We were just talking about the new set of twins Virginia Leigh adopted while she was out sick last week."

Almost instantaneously, Mr. Russell was the only one in the classroom who was not laughing. Everyone, including Mr. Russell, knew exactly what Preston was referring to and Preston, of course, ate the attention up.

"Alright," Mr. Russell started in, in an attempt to regain control of his class by removing the distraction. "Step out in the hall, Preston. I need to have a word with you. Or, more likely, several words."

Preston made it to his feet and headed for the door with pride as some of the laughter turned into a collective "Ooh" sound, in response to the fact that the class recognized Preston had gotten himself into trouble. Preston, on the other hand, continued to perform for his fellow students as laughter reclaimed its position as the dominant sound among his classmates. "Sure. You're probably thinking what I'm thinking. We should do an experiment on the fun-bags. Test the pressure or somethin'. You can put me in charge, Mr. Russell. I'm the right man for the job." Preston went back to making the international sign for boobs but cupped his hands much smaller as he was talking. "Too bad we don't have the before statistics to measure against the after." He expanded the cups to show the growth pattern of Virginia Leigh's assets. "All in the name of science, right? I think this is really smart of you, Mr. Russell. This is going to get the students a lot more engaged in science. You might win the teacher of the year award for this. They have that, right? You could even find yourself on the cover of *Educator Monthly*… If, of course, that's a real thing."

The entire classroom was hysterically cracking up with laughter as Mr. Russell and Preston stepped out into the hallway and the door closed behind them. The class watched through the tall but narrow window in the door as Mr. Russell indignantly scolded Preston.

Tyler was still chuckling as he looked down at his rocks. He casually reached forward to pick the igneous rock up. It briefly wiggled and then leapt into his hand. Startled, he sat back and glanced around the room to make sure no one else had seen it. Lucky for him, they were all preoccupied with *The Preston Show* going on in the hallway.

Setting the rock down, Tyler glanced around the room again to make sure no one was looking in his direction. He focused on the rock and tried to repeat the incident. Nothing happened. *Did I imagine it?* He found himself wondering as he continued to stare at the rock.

Suddenly, it leapt into his hand again and he quickly

scanned the room. *Phew,* he thought. *Still no gawkers.* He set it down and looked at the other two rocks. He reached forward and concentrated on the sedimentary rock. Almost immediately, the rock leapt into his hand the same way the igneous rock had. He quickly set that one down, too. He looked around the room again, as everyone else continued to watch Preston and Mr. Russell. Tyler tried like crazy not to think about the rocks anymore, glancing back at them a couple of times like someone trying to keep their eyes off of the giant wart on the nose of the person they're talking to.

Fear set in as he thought about his vision being restored overnight and added the rocks to his short mental list of odd happenings since he woke up this morning. The movie "Phenomenon", which he'd seen a year earlier at the local, one-screen movie theater, popped abruptly into his mind. The film starred John Travolta, Kyra Sedgwick, Forest Whitaker and Robert Duvall. Travolta's character had a fatal tumor on his brain that made some amazing things happen to him including super-intelligence and the same kind of telekinesis that Tyler was now experiencing with the rock. *Am I dying?* he suddenly wondered with his emotions teetering on panic. *I don't feel any smarter. Maybe that's a good thing,* he thought, trying to calm himself down.

Mr. Russell re-entered the classroom without Preston who gave everyone a quick wave as he started down the hallway on his way to the principal's office.

With the distraction of *The Preston Show* now over, Tyler quickly folded his hands in his lap and stared straight ahead to make sure nothing else happened that someone could bear witness to.

Looking down at his notes, Mr. Russell asked, "Now, where was I?"

"Ta-tas," a student announced to more chuckles.

"Alright," Mr. Russell started without any sign of amusement. "Who's funny guy number two? You people must really want to keep Principal McClean busy today. I assure you, he does not like having his time taken up with this kind of nonsensical behavior."

The only student in the classroom not giggling was Tyler.

The crowd funneled out of Mr. Russell's classroom, continuing to talk and laugh about the show Preston had just put on. Several of the students were even quoting Preston's suggestion of experiments and mimicking his demonstrative hand motions. From an outside perspective, one would think they had just been let out of a hilarious movie rather than an earth science class. Such was life in a world lived under the Preston effect.

At the back of the pack, still not laughing at all, was Preston's best friend, Tyler. He broke off from the crowd and walked quietly down the hallway to his locker. Deep concern over the incident with the rocks was still consuming his thoughts. On any other day, he would have laughed about Preston's antics as much as the rest of his classmates. After all, Preston had been his best friend almost his whole life for good reason. Today, however, was not like any other day he had ever experienced. At this moment, Preston wasn't even on his mind. While everyone else was thinking and talking about Preston, Tyler was understandably preoccupied with what was happening to him and he could only hope that he was the sole witness to the unexplainable events he had just experienced.

In the twenty-seven seconds it took for Tyler to reach his locker, he was able to ask himself some huge philosophical questions like *How and why did this happen to me?* but he was also thinking about all of the comic books he had read while growing up. The characters in those books were often humans who developed superpowers because they had been involved in some kind of an accident. But, nothing like that had happened to Tyler. This made it seem less random, which brought him right back to the questions *How and why did this happen to me?*

Standing in front of his locker, Tyler stared at the combination lock attached to the handle for a few seconds with no answers and no one to talk to. It was a frightening feeling. At least, it was frightening until his thoughts shifted gears and he began to ponder the immediate possibilities.

He glanced around to make sure no one was watching and then looked back at the lock. *Perhaps it's time for another test,* he thought before glancing around again, just to make sure that the coast was still clear. He slowly reached for the lock and it wiggled a bit, just like the igneous rock had. But, unlike the quick leap the rock had taken, the lock gradually rose from its resting position against the locker, signaling Tyler's gain of a bit more control. He deliberately lifted his hand up between the lock and the locker and watched as the lock gently dropped itself right into his hand.

Tyler exhaled and swallowed nervously as he looked around again, relieved and satisfied that no one had noticed. Gaining confidence, he lifted his other hand over the dial like he was going to turn it. But, before he even touched it, he decided to try something else. Sure enough, it began to turn for him. As Tyler's eyes slowly widened, the lock dialed the entire combination and then unlocked. He let go and jumped back, unsure if he should be excited or terrified; as the unlocked lock clanged noisily back down against the locker.

He stared at it for a moment, then looked around with a panicked feeling. A couple of students gave him a funny look, not because they knew what was happening, but because the noise had drawn their attention to the fact that Tyler was acting so strangely. He brushed it off and cautiously approached his locker again. He removed the lock and opened the door as a grin began to peek out of the corners of his mouth.

Suddenly, his moment of triumph was interrupted by a hand on his back that completely startled him. He nearly jumped out of his socks like someone in a cartoon. He spun around to find

Graham with two of his goons, Dan and Kevin, in tow.

"Hey Bert, where's Ernie?" Graham asked, laughing hard at his own joke.

"Always a pleasure Graham," Tyler responded, sarcastically. "Can I help you with something, or…?"

The smirk on Graham's face had quickly disappeared. "Yeah, you can stop looking at my girlfriend," he shouted venomously.

"Didn't realize I was." Tyler stated as he began to glance around. "In fact, I don't see Jessie anywhere."

Graham slammed Tyler up against his locker. "Don't get smart with me, Tommy."

"Tyler. And, I wasn't. I honestly didn't…"

He was interrupted when Jessie ran up and tried to push Graham off of him. "Leave him alone, Graham."

Graham suddenly let go of Tyler and turned to Jessie with a fake smile on his face.

"Found her," Tyler said, leaning toward Graham and pointing at Jessie.

After flashing Tyler a quick look to let him know he didn't appreciate the humor, Graham turned back toward Jessie to smooth things over. "Hey, baby. We were just having a chat. Weren't we, Tommy?"

"Yeah," Tyler answered. "Grimace and I… We were just having a chat. Always nice catching up."

Graham was furious at the fake name game Tyler had joined him in and the fact that Tyler's chosen name compared him to a fat, purple blob from the McDonald's gang. But, he couldn't do a thing about it. Instead, he swallowed hard as he stared at Tyler before turning his attention back to Jessie. "See," he exclaimed. "Just talkin'."

"Fine," Jessie imparted. "Then walk away."

"Yeah," Graham conceded. "Sure. I'm goin'." He kissed Jessie on the cheek, staring at Tyler to send a message of ownership, before walking away. "See you at lunch."

"See you at lunch," Jessie responded while watching him leave before turning her attention to Tyler. "Are you okay?"

"Never been better," Tyler responded, trying to hide the emotion he felt which fell somewhere between embarrassment and love on his imaginary psychological chart.

"I'm sorry. I don't know what gets into him sometimes."

"Probably steroids," Tyler uttered, only half joking. "I'm fine, Jessie. Really."

"Okay," Jessie replied before walking away with a bit of sorrow in her expression.

She was quickly replaced by Preston's arrival. "What happened? You look bricked. You're not gonna shout at your shoes, are ya?"

"Let it go, Preston," Tyler responded with a deep sadness

that had nothing to do with Preston and everything to do with Jessie. He exchanged his books and locked his locker – the same way he had done a thousand times and without resorting to any of the new tricks he was learning.

"Was Graham here?" Preston inquired, still trying to get to the bottom of Tyler's mood. "Did he rush you? We've gotta nuke that cheese-head."

"I'll see you at lunch," Tyler said as he walked away.

"We'll take care of this, Tyler," Preston announced as he watched his friend go. "Me and you. I promise." What Preston, unfortunately, didn't realize was that Tyler had suddenly found himself under a mountain of problems, not one of which Preston could possibly find a way to fix.

The schoolyard was packed with students eating their lunches. There were also a handful of teachers scattered about, supervising and making sure that peace and order were kept as much as could be reasonably expected. Especially at a small town public high school in the second half of the nineteen nineties.

Tyler and Preston sat underneath a tree, eating Mexican food from the school cafeteria, and Preston was continuing to have trouble letting go of the earlier situation with Graham. "I still can't believe that cob was joanin' you like that."

"Cob?" Tyler asked, puzzled. "Like, the salad or like corn on the…?"

"Alright," Preston admitted, "that one I made up. Works though, right?"

"Not even a little bit," Tyler said. "And, joanin's kind of ten years ago, don't you think?"

"Timeless," Preston insisted. "Just like it's namesake Joan Rivers. And stop avoiding the subject. Why do you think that duker was joanin' you so hard today?"

"Who knows?" Tyler imparted. "It's not the first time. Duker I like, by the way. Describes Graham to a tee. The only person I can think of that I'd like to flush down the toilet."

"Thank you," Preston said, accepting the praise. "And, yes, it does and I would, too. But, back to today. I know he's slammed you before. But, never without reason."

"What reason did he have before?"

"Well, you know, it's always been when he caught you scamming on Jessie. I thought we got out of there before he saw you bird-dogging this morning."

"I wasn't bird… When have I ever scammed on Jessie? Scamming involves flirting and that requires speaking. Until today, we haven't said more than ten words to each other since fifth grade."

"Duly noted," Preston declared. "But, you do gaze. And flirting is totally possible without speech. Otherwise mutes would never breed. Wait, you two talked today?"

"Yeah, she was the intermission between Graham and you."

"That's way more interesting than popcorn and jujubes in the lobby."

"When was the last time the movies had an intermission like

that?"

"Joan Rivers isn't the only thing that's timeless, Tyler. Roll with it. So, did Jesse come to your rescue or somethin'?"

"It wasn't like that."

"It totally was. No wonder you looked so bricked."

"I said it wasn't like that."

"Maybe not exactly like that. Because she's not the shining knight and you're no damsel. But, it was close and it still threw you. Totally understandable. I get it. Just keep in mind the obvious fact that we're not in fifth grade anymore. I know it's hard to separate the fact that the three of us were once best friends. But, she grew up, got hot, and bought the new and improved model from the friends aisle. Granted, it looks like her department store was more K-Mart and less Nordstrom but, I got over it and so did she. You're last in line, bro. And, it's been your turn for about half a decade now. Come on. Join the party of the real. Water's warm."

"You're crazy, man. I mean it. I can't keep up."

"You can't keep up? I'm not crazy. You're crazy. You're straight up loco in amor. I mean, we've established that she got hot. That's obvious. Whole school knows that. So, the lure is understandable. But, she flew the coup and left us to starve. Long time ago. Time to wake up and smell the trail of pretty perfume that leads into the forest of despair and then turn and run as fast as you can in the other direction before you get eaten by the prowling ravenous monsters."

"Prowling ravenous monsters? What are you talking about, man? You've completely lost me. But, I think it sounds like you're maybe the one that's in love with her."

"No way," Preston expressed before pondering a moment and then coming up with a revelation. "Her mom's crazy hot though."

"Oh, my…" Tyler whispered as he stared off in the distance.

"What? You just think it's gross because you want her to be your mother-in-law."

"I think you're gettin' a little ahead of yourself there, don't you?"

"Maybe. But, she is hot and you know it's true. She always has been. I swear she just keeps getting better. She's aging like a perfect Pinot Noir. Awesome."

"Like you've ever had a Pinot Noir," Tyler said, under his breath, as his eyes slowly scanned the school grounds. His stare was contemplative, with thoughts ranging from his relationship with Jesse as kids, and the lack thereof over the last decade, to the events of that very day. The contemplation lasted until he spotted two people several hundred yards away. They suddenly jumped into focus like they were five feet in front of him. It was Graham and Jessie and they were fighting over the fact that she had rushed to Tyler's defense in the hallway. "Jessie," Tyler said at a volume barely audible.

Jessie tried to apologize but Graham pushed her away so hard that she fell to the perfectly green grass and landed on her back, causing her eyes to bulge as she tried to catch her breath.

"No, not Jessie," Preston stated, oblivious to what Tyler was actually referring to. "Jessie's scorching hot mom. Are you even listening to me? You've got a one-track mind, bro. Jessie, Jessie, Jessie. All the time. Making Jessie a mantra won't make Jessie loving you a reality. I hope you know that."

"Leave her alone," Tyler stated emphatically as he got to his feet.

"Leave her alone?" Preston asked as he stared at his friend, confused as to why Tyler was now standing up. "Is my attraction to her mom hurting her in some way? Or, do you just need her to be the damsel in distress now so you can be the knight in shining armor? Maybe you're the one that needs to leave her alone. Ever think about that? You're the one with the crazy obsession, dude. And, what the heck are you lookin' at over there?" Preston asked, finally realizing they might not be on the same page. He looked to see what Tyler was staring at. "What's down there, fry-daddy?"

Graham grabbed Jessie by the arm, hard, and pulled her to her feet. He continued to scold her for sticking up for Tyler. She was clearly scared and in pain.

"He's hurting her," Tyler announced quietly but angrily.

Preston was still looking but it was so far away he couldn't tell exactly what it was he was looking at. "What are you talking about, buddy? Someone's actually, physically hurting Jessie? Tell me what you're talking about. Who's hurting her? And why do I feel like I'm talkin' to Lassie?"

"Graham."

"Graham's hurting her? Oh, I'll put the smack down on his A-bomb. You rush him and I'll come in behind you for the kill. Wait. Where? Where do you see this, Joe Broseph?"

"Football field."

"What?" Preston probed. "I think I can see something down there but, I can't tell what it is. There's no way you can see that far."

"Something weird is happening to me," Tyler admitted.

"No kidding."

"I can't explain it."

"I can explain it," Preston told him while glancing at Tyler's lunch and then back up at Tyler himself. "You're hallucinating, homie. Maybe you got a bad burrito."

"I'm not hallucinating. I've got to do somethin'."

"Like what?"

"What I should've done a long time ago. This ends now."

CHAPTER NINE
Escalation

Like a heavy square rock would awkwardly emerge from the quick release of a slingshot, Tyler took off as fast as any non-athletic teenaged boy possibly could. He raced toward the football field with determination in every pump of his arms, retribution in the pounding of every step, and a decade of unrequited love in every breath of air in his lungs. This was finally his moment to take a stand both against Graham and for Jessie, and he was going to take full advantage of it regardless of the consequences.

"What you should have…" Preston pondered momentarily while he sat alone in the confusing wake of Tyler's sudden departure. "What does that mean?" Finally, Preston realized that Tyler meant he was about to confront Graham. He still couldn't figure out how Tyler knew Graham and Jessie were even on the football field. Fear immediately set in and quickly escalated to a state of panic that arrived with all the subtlety of the school's marching band. "Oh, no you don't. That smack down thing was just an act. We can't rush… Tyler, come back. It's suicide, man. Tyler! TYLER!"

Preston's head swiveled in flustered uncertainty as Tyler pressed on, so focused he didn't even hear his friend's incessant yelling. Preston finally hurried over to a tall and lanky teacher with thin-framed glasses and a clean-shaven face. "Mr. Brooks!" Preston shouted. "Graham is going to beat the crap out of both Tyler and Jessie."

"What?" Mr. Brooks asked with puzzlement quickly shifting into a deep concern. "Wait. What? What's going on? A fight?"

"They're down on the football field," Preston exclaimed. "Just check it out before somebody dies."

"You know," Mr. Brooks hesitated, having had a few seconds to think about who he was talking to, "you've tricked me before, Preston. Are you trying to get me to leave the area so you can pull one of your pranks? You know, I still get flack from pretty much the entire staff about the time you convinced me that the vending machines had all-"

"Mr. Brooks…" Preston interrupted, begging with a discernable sincerity that was rarely seen on his typically cunning face. "Please."

Mr. Brooks quickly lifted a walkie-talkie to his mouth. He

had thought of a way to maintain his post while still checking out the fight. But, he was still a bit wary of Preston and his motivations. So, before triggering the microphone, he gave Preston one more stern warning: "You make me regret this even a little bit, Preston, and I'll have you cleaning toilets with a toothbrush for detention until you graduate. I might even try to find a way to turn it into a Summer program for all the stunts you pulled before."

"I won't. I promise."

"Bailey, are you available?"

From the other end of the walkie-talkie, Bailey quickly responded, "Sure. Who's this and what's up?"

"This is Carl Brooks. I've got a possible conflict on the football field. Can you look into it for me?"

"I'm on it."

"Thanks, Mr. Brooks." Preston said, earnestly, before running off toward the football field to catch up with Tyler.

Meanwhile, Tyler arrived at the scene of the ongoing confrontation. He stared single-mindedly at Graham and Jessie as he stepped out onto the football field just in time to watch Graham pull Jessie to within an inch of his chest as he continued to yell at her.

"I swear to God," Graham shouted maliciously, "if you ever embarrass me in front of my friends like that again I'll-"

"You'll what?" Tyler interrupted to Graham's surprise. "You'll what, Graham? Are you threatening to hurt her?"

Graham let go of Jessie with a little shove and turned toward Tyler, delighted to have another chance to pummel his face in, as Jessie stumbled a few steps, trying to catch her balance. "Oh, speak of the devil…" Graham began. "She came to your rescue this morning and now you're coming to hers. How cute. You're a real match made in heaven, aren't you? How freaking adorable. You're just like a couple of precious little puppies. I hope you two have had fun because your playtime is over. Now it's my turn. And, I've been waiting a long time for this, pal."

"You can do whatever you want to me," Tyler insisted. "Just leave Jessie alone."

"Or, what, hero?"

"Find out."

"I intend to," Graham said forcefully before diverting his eyes to Jessie. "Clark Kent over here wants to be your Superman, Jessie. Should we find out what's underneath that cape? Or, do you already know?"

"Just leave, Graham," Jessie pleaded. "Please."

"I don't think so," Graham said vigorously as he charged toward Tyler. "Let's skip her and get right to you and me."

"Is that a romantic offer, Graham?" Tyler asked without flinching as Graham pulled his fist back to his shoulder, about to throw a punch.

"That's enough, Graham!" Bailey shouted as he jogged up, intruding on Graham's fun. Bailey was a short, out-of-shape, forty-five year old groundskeeper who was huffing and puffing pretty heavily from his short jaunt to the field.

Graham knew he could take him, and considered it, but wised up to the fact that the consequences of such an action just weren't worth it. He'd have to be patient. But, revenge was coming. He was determined to make sure of it.

"You tattled on me?" Graham yelled at Tyler. "Some Superman." Graham turned his attention to Bailey, "Why are you assuming it was me? How do you know Tommy didn't start this but tattle on me first as some kind of a set-up?"

"Because my brain is a lot bigger than that tiny little thing rattling around in your skull," Bailey fired back. "Now, come on. Let's go. Otherwise, I'll have to involve the police. Neither of us wants that hassle."

"Why not, Bailey?" Graham inquired like a wise guy. "You got a record?"

"Not yet, I don't," Bailey answered. "But, keep talkin'. I might by the time this conversation is over."

Bailey and Graham walked away as Tyler smiled at Jessie before turning to leave.

"Tyler," Jessie said to get his attention.

"Yeah?" Tyler responded as he turned around.

"Thanks."

"Yeah," he said as he turned back. "Just returning the favor."

"No need. And, you don't have to worry about me."

"I think I do," he told her without looking back as he walked away.

"Just be careful," Jessie petitioned. "Graham can be pretty scary when he's mad."

"I've noticed," Tyler said under his breath as he kept walking, ultimately joining Preston who showed up just in time to do absolutely nothing.

"Everything okay?" Preston inquired.

"Fine," Tyler lied as he felt the weight of his problems mounting to a level he had never imagined possible. The day was only half over and it was already the most eventful day he'd ever had. Some good, some bad, some just downright confusing. His concern, however, was that the events in the first half of the day would pale in comparison to those in the second. He was, of course, absolutely right. What he couldn't possibly know, however, was that those later events would have grave consequences.

CHAPTER TEN
Trouble Brewing

In a classroom decorated with maps and pictures of George Washington, Abraham Lincoln, and other American historical figures, Mr. Brooks stood at the front, facing the students. He was clearly fascinated by the topic of his own lecture. As he spoke, the depiction of a woman being burned at the stake was being projected on the white board behind him. "In all, about a hundred and fifty people were accused of witchcraft in Salem and nearby Andover, Massachusetts between 1692 and 1693. But, much of what you've heard is nothing more than distorted folklore. For example, only about twenty of the accused were really executed and, the truth is, not a single one of them was actually burned at the stake. They were all hanged like common criminals. Plus, not all of the people executed were women. About a quarter of them were men and, as if to prove that fact is sometimes stranger than fiction, two of them were canines."

"Dogs?" a student asked in complete shock.

"Dogs," Mr. Brooks answered, proud to know he had the attention of his students. Of course, that could not be said for all of his students.

While a lecture about people suffering because of fear over misunderstanding is something that may have been useful to Tyler in his current circumstances, he and Preston, per their routine, sat in the back corner of the classroom once again paying more attention to each other than to their teacher. Some of the information, however, did seep into Tyler's brain and would inevitably influence his decision to keep the things that were happening to him a secret. But, his slightly divided attention, at the moment, was primarily focused on Preston and the anticipated problem represented by the pot of anger boiling over inside of Graham.

"All I'm sayin' is," Preston persisted, "after what happened at lunch, Graham is going to be ten times as agro as he was when you were just scammin' his Betty."

"I was never scamming his Betty," Tyler insisted. "How many times do we have to go over that?"

"Okay," Preston conceded, "for arguments sake, let's say you weren't. Even though you totally were." Before Tyler could interject his rebuttal, Preston conceded again in the interest of moving forward. "But let's say you weren't. What really matters is that he thinks you were."

"I guess that's fair," Tyler acknowledged.

"But, now you've dissed him in front of Jessie. He's got to pick up his face after an incident like this. And, there's not a shred of doubt in anyone's mind that you've been tagged as his target. You've moved up to the top of his most wanted list."

"I get it."

"Let's make sure," Preston continued. He motioned for Tyler to look across the back row of students. "Look over there for me."

Tyler leaned forward and looked down the row. His line of vision reached the end and he locked eyes with Graham who was staring right at him with anger so furious Tyler could almost see the cartoon steam billowing out from his ears. A nervous look crossed Tyler's face before he jumped back and looked at Preston.

"That man is full of acid and ready to front," Preston stated with anxiety in his voice. "You know what I'm sayin'?

"Do you?" Tyler asked sincerely.

Ignoring Tyler's question, Preston continued. "I can't believe you slammed him like that. I mean, don't get me wrong, I'm all for nukin' the cheese-wiener, but catch him when he's not lookin'. Maybe, I don't know, fork his lawn or somethin'."

"Wouldn't that be punishing his parents more than him?"

"They produced him."

"True," Tyler admitted, " but that wouldn't exactly help Jessie."

"This isn't about Jessie," Preston insisted out of pure frustration. "Why do you want to help that traitor, anyway? What has she done for you lately?"

"Listen, Janet Jackson. Jessie's not a traitor, it is about helping her, and helping a friend has nothing to do with what she's done for me or when she did it."

"It has everything to do with it. The guy's a spud. No question. But, you cut on him. Now he has his game face on and you're in la la land for a Betty that traded you in. You're a very handsome pony, by the way. But, she traded you in for a Clydesdale. You're risking getting' pureed over a girl who ditched us both for a better life like six years ago. Get it together, man. You're in danger here. And, for what? For Jessie? That old crush is totally played out. If I were you, I'd skip town pronto. It ain't worth it, amigo."

"Now you're Mexican. I can't keep up."

"You're a dead man in any language. Can you keep up with that? And, for the record, you might want to think about literally making a run for the border."

"Taco Bell?"

"Mexico," Preston insisted as loudly as he could without

drawing the attention of Mr. Brooks.

"I hear you loud and clear. And, thanks for the pep talk, by the way. So helpful."

"I just hope you're listening."

The final school bell rang and the seed of fear planted in Tyler earlier in the day began to take root. He and Preston followed the crowd out of the classroom and Graham filed in a few people behind them.

"I got it, Preston," Tyler stated with a tinge of frustration in his voice.

"I'm not joshin' about this," Preston whispered to Tyler as they entered the hallway. "And, neither is Graham. In fact, why don't you come over to my house tonight? I'm gonna get my dad to hook you up with a life insurance policy."

Graham suddenly hurried up behind Tyler and shouldered him into a row of lockers like a linebacker knocking a running back out of bounds. "You're a dead man, Tommy."

"Tyler," Tyler corrected in a whisper barely audible to anyone but himself. "You're a dead man, Tyler."

Preston stared at Tyler and shook his head disapprovingly. "I rest my case."

"First of all, I'm not on trial. And, second, I already told you I read you loud and clear. I'd have to be completely deaf to not get it by now. You're like a living bullhorn. Besides, he's just trying to scare me," Tyler said unconvincingly.

"Is it working?"

"Oh yeah, it's working."

"Good. What are you gonna do about it?"

"Nothing."

"Nice. Solid plan. Good luck with that."

"What am I supposed to do?"

"I already told you to skip town," Preston said as he began to hum *La Bamba* and dance.

"If I needed to leave the country," Tyler quickly interrupted, "I'd go to Canada. Way closer."

"Not the point," Preston insisted.

"Not an option," Tyler fired back.

"Then," Preston started as he stopped his mariachi impression and pulled out his wallet. He fished out a business card to offer Tyler, "call my dad. Seriously. I don't think this can wait until dinner. His work number is right there. He'll hook you up with a primo life insurance policy. Young healthy dude like you will get off cheap. Besides, the least you could do is leave your mom a couple of million bucks. Forget I said that, make me your beneficiary."

Tyler stared at Preston blankly.

"What? I'm your best friend." Tyler walked away while, as usual, Preston continued running his mouth. "That has to be worth something. I should be compensated while I'm in the grieving process. Call my Dad, Tyler! Seriously! He'll hook you up!"

CHAPTER ELEVEN

...And Ears To Hear

Tyler and Preston returned to the parking lot for the first time since that morning. Tyler was carrying his usual backpack full of books and Preston, as was his routine, was carrying a whole lot of nothing. Of course, the only thing on either one of their minds as they approached their cars was the dramatic events of the day. The main difference in the way the two of them were handling it was, as one might expect, Tyler didn't want to talk about it and Preston couldn't turn off the motor that was his mouth.

"I have to ask one more thing," Preston said inquiringly.

"What?" Tyler responded with a deep sigh, reluctantly giving him a wide open door.

"How in the world did you ever see what was going down on the football field today? That was hundreds and hundreds of yards away. There's not a person on this planet that could have seen anything clearly from that far away. You knew who it was and what was going on. Come on. Please. Explain that to me."

"There's nothing to explain. I'm sure lots of people-"

"No one," Preston interrupted.

"Maybe you should get contacts," Tyler said with a grin sprouting as he pointed to his own eyes. "Or, at least put some lenses in those Urkel frames on your face."

"Urkel?" Preston responded in dismay. "More like Weezer. Don't be disrespecting the frames if you want backup when Graham decides the time has finally come to smash up your grill."

"My sincerest apologies."

"And they are accepted. Now, about the football field…"

"What am I supposed to tell you, Preston?"

"How?"

"Don't know. Just saw it."

"But, how?"

Tyler stared at Preston blankly.

"I'll accept the fact that you don't know," Preston finally compromised.

"Thank you for believing I'm not a liar," Tyler said without an ounce of sincerity.

"But, why then, do you not seem the least bit curious?"

"About what?"

"About how it happened!"

"I guess I just don't see why it's such a big deal," Tyler lied without the hypocrisy of having just thanked his best friend for believing he wasn't a liar escaping him. "I already tried to tell you I think lots of people-"

"No one," Preston interrupted again with an unrelenting stare. After about three seconds of silence, Preston threw his hands dramatically up in the air and exhaled with enough power to dwarf Tyler's previous sigh. "Fine. Whatever. I give up. You win. You're Fort Knox."

"I'm not Fort Knox. I just don't have anything to tell you."

"Like I said, you win."

"Excellent. Later."

"Lates."

Tyler and Preston quickly did the four-part high-five in the shape of a big X that started at eye level and went below Tyler's waistline that they had been doing nearly every time they parted, ever since the fourth grade. As soon as that was complete, Tyler climbed into his truck and shut the door. He sat in silence for a moment as Preston climbed into his car, still baffled by Tyler's ability to see clearly what was happening on the football field from such a distance.

Secretly perplexed by the day's events as well, Tyler just wanted to go home and be by himself to figure things out. Of course, he felt the need to figure out what was happening to him.

But, he also wanted to try and figure out how to fix things for Jessie. He wanted to protect her, even if she said she didn't need it. Whether she was right or not had nothing to do with it. He wanted to be there for her. Jessie and his mom were the two people Tyler cared most about in the world. His crazy friend Preston would be a close third on that list. Sadly, no one else even came close enough to call them fourth. It was a short list, but an important one. Maybe that's why he was never quite able to let Jessie slip off of it.

Pushing the clutch in with his left foot and putting the key in the ignition to start his car, he looked in his rearview mirror and spotted two of Jessie's friends, Andrea and Liz, talking in a red Honda Civic parked in the row of cars behind him. Suddenly, he let off of the clutch and released the keys as their voices became audible with stunning clarity.

"I mean who does she think she is asking him to Sadie Hawkins?" Andrea proposed. "She's so Brady."

Shocked by the fact that the conversation suddenly sounded like it could be taking place just couple of feet away, Tyler spun around in his seat to get a better look as Preston fired up his Fuego and drove away. Tyler was able to zoom in on the faces of the girls in the red Civic as if his eyes were telephoto lenses. The girls' words definitely matched their moving lips. He zoomed back out and glanced around his truck. His windows were rolled up, as were the windows in the Civic. His radio wasn't on so, there was absolutely no doubt left that it was their voices. But, as he spun back around to take another look and listen, he couldn't figure out why he was hearing them at all.

"I mean of course he said no because he knew I would eventually ask him," Andrea continued. "We've been flirting for like two weeks. Hello?"

"I went through the same thing with Mindy Widen," Liz shot back. "She tried to get George to go and of course he was like, no way, you're crusin' in the wrong direction, but still."

Andrea suddenly spotted Tyler and pointed him out. "Is that guy looking at us?"

"He is," Liz agreed. "Eww."

"Yeah. Gross."

Tyler spun back around and started his engine. He slammed his truck into reverse, pulled out of the parking space, popped it into first gear and took off in a hurry. Having been spotted staring at Andrea and Liz would have normally embarrassed Tyler to the nth degree but today he felt no embarrassment. He was far too concerned about people finding out what was going on with him. And, he was even more worried about figuring out for himself exactly what it was that was happening to him. Even Jessie's problems temporarily left his thoughts.

What is happening to me? He wondered to himself over and

over again as he sped toward home, wanting to get there and be alone even more than he had sixty seconds earlier.

Although Tyler wouldn't have thought things could possibly get any more bizarre than they had already been that morning and the first part of the afternoon, he was well aware of the fact that the biggest danger he currently faced was running into Graham. He hoped that leaving the school reduced his chances of that happening but would soon find out that he was wrong. That run-in would spur on the craziest part of his day and it was now just a few moments away.

CHAPTER TWELVE
ROAD RAGE

Cemetery by the Australian alternative rock band Silverchair had just begun playing on the radio as Tyler drove his truck to the end of the country road. He pulled up to a stop sign that had been plastered with over half a dozen "102.1 The Quake: Central Washington's Rock Station" stickers and one yellow Nirvana smiley face sticker. Tyler made a nearly complete stop before making a right hand turn onto the two-lane highway.

Although the winter chill was in the air, there was no snow on the ground and the bright sunshine coupled with the desert landscape on both sides of the highway was a clear indicator that Penuel was East of the Cascade Mountain Range. The lack of traffic was a reminder that the closest town of significant size was Ellensburg. Even that only had a population of about 15,000 and was nearly fifty miles away. Wenatchee was almost double the size of Ellensburg but the drive was also an additional twenty miles. Both were West of Penuel. Ellensburg was even West of the Columbia River and also to the South of Penuel while Wenatchee had the Columbia River running right through it and was to the North of Penuel.

Tyler sang along with Silverchair as Graham's car approached menacingly from behind in the distance. Graham's timing was not perfect enough to make this happen without some planning. He had left school, immediately after the final bell had rung, to make a grocery store run. After he got what he needed at the store, he had parked on the side of the highway, just far enough east of the stop sign. He knew Tyler would have to enter the highway at that intersection on his way home, and waited until he saw Tyler's red truck. But, his wait was only a few minutes and if Tyler had been able to get Preston to stop talking in the parking lot, Graham may have missed him altogether that day. But, Tyler, in this particular case, was not so lucky.

He was attempting to zone out and let go of the events that had been occurring since he woke up that morning. He just wanted to get home and spend some time alone before his mom arrived. It was nothing against his mom. He just needed some time to process everything. Tyler knew he would have plenty of opportunity to worry about all of the outrageous and seemingly unexplainable things that were taking place in his body during those two hours or so he would have to himself in the solace of his home. He needed it. But, at this moment, he needed to try and forget about all of it before the massive processing session that would undoubtedly follow. He had even considered taking a nap when he got home and briefly wondered if he could wake up and discover that this had all just been a terrible but thrilling dream. If only it was all that simple…

Singing at the top of his lungs, Tyler was unaware of Graham's presence at first but eventually glanced up at his rearview mirror and the black Camaro caught his eye. Tyler spun around as Graham continued to pick up speed and close in on Tyler's truck. He whirled back around to look at the road even though he couldn't help repeatedly glancing up at the rearview mirror as Graham moved closer. By the time Tyler reached his fifth glance, Graham was close enough to start waving with a big, cocky grin on his face.

Once Tyler finally noticed that Dan and Kevin were both with him, Graham swung his car over the broken yellow line into the empty oncoming traffic lane and sped up alongside Tyler's truck. Tyler looked to his left and nervously watched Graham's approach in his side mirror until the two vehicles were parallel.

While Dan and Kevin both gave Tyler the middle finger out of the open passenger side window, Graham swerved his car at Tyler's truck. Fear had not only taken root inside of Tyler at this point, it was now completely taking over.

Suddenly, both Tyler and Graham spotted an oncoming eighteen-wheeler. Tyler let off the gas as Graham sped up and cut Tyler off, sliding out of the way of the massive truck without so much as a second to spare.

"Okay," Graham told his friends, "time to bust out the goods."

Kevin obeyed his leader. Sitting in the back seat, he picked a plastic bag up off of the floor. He reached inside and pulled out a carton of eggs as Graham rolled down the driver's side window.

Tyler watched as arms with white dots in their hands popped out of windows on both sides of the car. Suddenly, he noticed that something was thrown from each side because the hands jerked and released. The white dots he'd spotted swiftly increased in size until...

SPLAT!

SPLAT!

The eggs connected with Tyler's windshield and spread their goo all over it.

SPLAT!

SPLAT!

More eggs and more goo.

Flipping the windshield wipers on, Tyler watched as the goo smeared all over the place. Quickly collecting dust from the air, the smeared eggs got darker and heavier as visibility became virtually non-existent.

With the eighteen-wheeler now gone, Graham swerved back into the on-coming traffic lane to fall back in parallel with Tyler again. Dan and Kevin immediately bombarded the driver side window with eggs.

SPLAT! SPLAT!

SPLAT! SPLAT!

Tyler could no longer see anything either to his left or in front of him. He was essentially driving blind.

Graham spotted an approaching car. He sped up and cut Tyler off again but, as soon as he settled into the lane, a possum ran across the highway. Graham, naturally, hit his brakes as hard as a wrecking ball to an abandoned building.

All Tyler could see was a big red glare. He recognized it as brake lights and yanked the steering wheel left to swerve away from the light. There was no way for him to know that he was swerving right in front of an oncoming car.

The driver of the oncoming car was Nancy Hanley, a seventy-eight year-old mother of four, grandmother of ten, great-grandmother of two, and widow of one. When she saw Tyler's truck swerve in front of her less than one hundred feet away, her instinct was to raise her hands and shield herself.

Silverchair's *Cemetery* continued blaring from the truck's stereo speakers.

CRASH!

The head-on collision was catastrophic. Both vehicles folded like origami and sailed off the highway onto opposite sides of the road.

WHAM-WHUMP! WHAM-WHUMP! WHAM-WHUMP! WHAM-WHUMP! WHAM-WHUMP! WHAM-WHUMP!

Each vehicle rolled over and over again until finally stopping a little less than a football field away from one another. During the fourth flip of his truck, Tyler was launched through the windshield and landed in the dirt with an abrupt thud.

Graham hit the brakes again and skidded his black Camaro to a complete stop. He looked at the wreckage with terror and remorse, knowing in his heart that no one could have survived.

CHAPTER THIRTEEN
Restoration

"What do we do now?" Kevin squealed from the backseat as both he and Dan started to come to grips with the horror that they had caused. As the full-fledged feelings of panic took hold, they realized they were responsible for the likely deaths of two people and both of them began to tremble with fear.

Graham, on the other hand, had the exact opposite reaction to that of his partners in this dreadful, albeit somewhat accidental, crime. He didn't utter a sound or move a muscle. He felt incapable of doing anything. So, for what felt like several minutes, but was really only a few seconds, he simply sat still in completely stunned silence.

Had they been separate places, the back seat of the black Camaro would have sounded like an insane asylum that had run out of calming meds for the patients and the front seat would have seemed more like a college campus library during finals week. But, this was one location with such contrasting responses to the same situation that, for those few seconds where Graham remained shell-shocked, it felt like a living paradox.

"We just killed two people," added Dan. "We're goin' to Walla Walla, man!"

"I can't go to prison," Kevin gasped. "I'll never survive. I'm way too cute. Graham! We can't go to prison, man! We can't let it happen. We have to do something. What do we do?"

Graham, still silent and barely moving, finally looked around. He looked at both cars. The road was raised and the desert sloped down before plateauing. So, each of the wrecked vehicles rested at least twenty feet below street level. Next, Graham looked both in front of him and behind him. The highway was empty.

"What do we do?" repeated Kevin. "We can't go down for this, Graham! We can't-"

"Let me think," Graham finally spoke, quietly but firmly interrupting Kevin's tirade.

"Think about what, man?" Dan asked frantically.

"No one except the two people who are already dead saw anything," Graham said, looking around again to make sure. Still completely frantic, both Dan and Kevin looked around and started to agree with his assessment.

"He's right," Kevin decided out loud as a hint of calm began to creep in. "Let's just get out of here."

"We can't just leave," Dan contended. "We just killed two people."

"Staying's not gonna bring 'em back to life," Kevin insisted. "Come on! Let's just get out of here. No one will ever know we were even here. Use your head, man. It's this or prison. Do you want to be some thug's girlfriend? I know I sure don't. So, I vote we go."

A brief moment of silence, that once again felt like minutes, is all it took for all three teenagers to make the spineless decision to save themselves and flee the scene of the crime instead of checking to see if either Tyler or Nancy were alive. In the end, the risk of facing the consequences of their actions was too much for any of them to handle.

"You're right," Dan finally agreed. "Just do it. Just go. Get out of here before I change my mind."

Without another word, Graham peeled out and sped away. Once the Camaro was out of earshot, both the highway and the inside of the wrecked cars sounded like the library.

Nancy was a bloody mess and showing no signs of life. Her gold 1976 Pontiac Grand Prix LJ had rolled back onto its wheels but it was so smashed up it had shrunk to about a third of its original size.

Tyler's truck was a disaster too. The roof, front, back and sides were all caved in. Luckily, he had been thrown out of the truck and, although he looked to be in as bad of shape as Nancy, he slowly regained consciousness.

The pain immediately set in and Tyler started to groan and grimace as his fists clinched the dirt and his eyes gradually opened. He noticed a warm feeling inside and considered the possibility that he had a fever. Sitting up, he brushed the dirt out of his hands, shook the dirt out of his hair, and wiped his face clean as his eyes adjusted, just like they would if he had was awakening from a long, hard sleep. He looked at his injuries as well as his surroundings and knew immediately that the accident had been severe.

Just being alive seemed miraculous but the miracle wasn't over. As what he suspected was a fever heated up inside of him, Tyler watched his bloody and bruised body begin to heal itself. Pieces of glass fell from his skin and wounds began to heal. His skin closed up, forming scar tissue which gradually turned from pink into his normal skin color, leaving only the blood and tears in his clothes as evidence of the injuries he had suffered.

Tyler's eyes widened as he witnessed the miraculous healing that was taking place. Even the pain he felt was disappearing. *How is this possible?* he wondered.

As he regained his composure, Tyler got to his feet and stood back for a moment to survey the damage. He shook his legs, rolled his neck and shrugged his shoulders. The fact that he no longer felt any pain, and even the fever had left him, was utterly mystifying. But, it was real.

Suddenly, he remembered that another car had been involved. He assumed it was Graham's Camaro at first, but then wondered whose brake lights he had swerved away from. *Was there a third car?* he pondered. He spun in circles and looked all around him but saw no other cars, let alone two others. He ran up to the side of the highway and finally spotted a car on the other side of the road. It wasn't Graham's. He glanced both up and down the highway and briefly thought about what a coward Graham was. Tyler ran across the highway and quickly down to the car. He could see Nancy in the driver's seat and ran up to the passenger side, climbing in, as another car finally approached on the highway and stopped. A man quickly got out with a large cellular phone pressed to his ear.

"Hey," he yelled, gaining Tyler's attention. "You okay down there?"

"I am," Tyler answered, "but this woman's hurt! Call an ambulance!"

"On it!" the man responded and then quietly spoke into the phone. "Uh, baby, I'm gonna have to call you back."

Tyler put his ear over Nancy's mouth to see if she was breathing. Nothing. He checked her pulse. Nothing. He sat back in grief over a woman he'd never even seen before. *She's dead*, he thought.

Out of nowhere, he began to feel an energy course through his body. The fever was returning. But, it quickly pooled in his hands. *Maybe this isn't a fever,* he contemplated. Whatever it was, it felt like it was causing his hands to want to extend outward over Nancy's body and he wasn't about to fight them. He placed one on her forehead and the other on her knee.

Her wounds began to heal the same way his had. As pieces of glass fell from her skin and both new scar tissue and bruises lost their coloring, the blood, tears and stains in her clothing became the only evidence of injuries – just the way it had happened with Tyler.

Tyler heated up even further as he felt the loss of energy from his body. It wore on him and a slight light-headedness set in.

Nancy's lungs filled with air and she sat forward. "Tyler," she spoke as if it were a natural reaction to the return of life.

Tyler fell backwards, partly frightened by the response and partly because he lacked the energy to hold himself up. Now, out of the car, he sat in the dirt and looked at the stranger who had just spoken his name. "What did you just say?" he asked.

Nancy looked him in the eyes and smiled. She spoke with warmth, sincerity, and confidence. "Tyler. You're Tyler. They told me you would bring me back."

"Who told you?"

"The angels, of course."

CHAPTER FOURTEEN
St. Tyler

The accident scene was now active with an ambulance and its medics, two tow-trucks and their drivers, and several police cars and the officers that came with them including the man in charge, Sheriff Ron Wilson. Detours had been set up to redirect traffic and the highway was completely blocked off for close to a quarter of a mile on either side of the site. The police vehicles were parked on the highway, taking up both lanes, adding an additional barrier so no one could reach the scene. Two of the police officers were taking pictures of tire tracks and pieces of debris from the accident.

The ambulance and tow trucks, along with the rest of the personnel, were all off the road, however. One of the tow trucks was parked near Tyler's truck and both the other tow truck and the ambulance were near Nancy's car. Other than the medics and the accident victims, those who weren't directing traffic were all surveying the damaged vehicles.

The emergency response vehicles were all a little out of date for 1997. Most police precincts replace their squad cars every couple of years as the vehicles approach the 65,000 mile mark. The police cars in Penuel were nine years old. The ambulance that had been dispatched from the fire station was more than twice that age. The tow-trucks at the scene were the newest vehicles there. One was seven years old and the other was only three.

Sheriff Wilson was in his late forties and a "lifer" in Penuel. He was a decent looking man but, not in a typical movie star way. He looked a bit weathered and about as much like a cowboy as a man can without the customary hat and boots. He had long reminded Tyler of Sam Elliott, who had just appeared in one of Tyler's favorite movies, *Tombstone*, only a few years earlier, even though he lacked the lip sweater and had a slightly rounder face. His heart was softer than the shell that carried it. That was reflected in the genuine respect he showed the people he came into contact with, particularly the people of the town he took pride in caring for and protecting.

Surveying the scene in disbelief, the sheriff observed that both vehicles were completely destroyed. Yet, no one had been killed. His gaze panned the terrain on its way over to the back of the ambulance where both Tyler and Nancy sat. The sheriff knew

Nancy a little bit. He was aware that she was a widow with children and grandchildren. But, he didn't know her well. However, he was very familiar with Tyler because he had been in love with Tyler's mom for years, dating back to her days working with Gwen in the diner. His history with Kathleen pre-dated Tyler's birth so, Sheriff Wilson had watched the boy grow up from the start. He had never married or had children of his own and had long since blamed his own inhibition and lack of assertiveness for letting Kathleen get away. That happened when she linked up with Brett Riggle. He had even wished, from time to time, that he could have been Tyler's father.

As he approached the ambulance, the sheriff experienced a bit of caution. His feelings for Kathleen and Tyler put him in an awkward position. He was especially concerned for Tyler's well-being and for Kathleen's emotional state when she would eventually find out what her son had been through. But, as the sheriff in Penuel, he needed to remain professional and not let those feelings show. He also needed to find the truth about how this accident had happened and could not allow anything to stand in the way of that goal. He was a good man who wanted to do the right thing and, more often than not, the right thing is exactly what Ron Wilson did.

With Tyler and Nancy coming into closer view, the sheriff immediately noticed that Nancy appeared peaceful and calm while Tyler looked to be completely shocked by what he had just lived through. "Everybody okay over here?" the sheriff asked routinely.

"I've never been better," Nancy quickly piped up.

Beginning to wonder if Nancy was just in a different kind of shock, the sheriff inquired further. "That's kind of strange considering the circumstances, don't you think?"

"Sheriff," Nancy gleefully responded, "we're in the presence of an angel."

Looking around and wondering how hard Nancy had hit her head, the sheriff asked, "We are?"

"Right here," Nancy stated in a tone that sounded as if she was insinuating that the sheriff was wasting his time looking anywhere else. Just to emphasize where he should be looking, she gave Tyler's leg a little pat.

"You mean Tyler?" the sheriff asked in disbelief.

"Yes," Nancy stated emphatically and full of hope that the sheriff was finally getting it.

Instead, the sheriff pressed further. "Do you mean to say Tyler was heroic?"

"No," Nancy insisted. "I mean Tyler is a real, live angel from Heaven.

The sheriff chuckled a bit before stating, "With all due respect, ma'am, I've known Tyler his whole life. He's a good kid, but he's no angel." The sheriff turned to Tyler, still fighting the urge to laugh, and asked, "Are you hearing this, Tyler?" After waiting for a response and not getting one, the sheriff's concern increased. "Tyler?"

"He's special," Nancy insisted as she took mental note of Tyler's current state of distress. She found Tyler's state peculiar for an angel and couldn't help but let a bit of doubt overtake her previous conviction. Feeling a bit embarrassed, Nancy caved in a little to the pressure without relenting completely. "Angel or not, he's not like you and me, Sheriff."

Ignoring Nancy, the sheriff raised his voice to get the attention of one of the medics. "Hey, we've got a kid in shock over here." He stepped over to the medic and spoke quietly so Nancy couldn't hear him. "In fact, I think we have two accident victims in shock. I want you to get them both to Kittitas Valley immediately and have them completely checked out."

"You've got it, Sheriff," the medic agreed.

The sheriff walked the medic back over to Tyler and Nancy, addressing them. "They're going to take you to Ellensburg now and have you looked over just as a precaution. Tyler, I'll swing by the bank on my way over there and pick up your mother."

The medics helped Tyler and Nancy climb back inside the ambulance and closed the back doors. The sheriff watched as the ambulance drove away. He looked back at the wreckage on either side of the highway. As a deputy for more than twenty years and then the sheriff of Penuel for the last four, he'd seen a lot of car accidents. This was one of the worst and he couldn't figure out how either Tyler or Nancy had walked away from it. Even more, it was nothing short of a miracle that both of them had. What Nancy said about Tyler sounded totally crazy. But, it was evident that something was off about this whole event. He just didn't know what it was. But, good cops know how to find the truth and Sheriff Ron Wilson was a really good cop.

CHAPTER FIFTEEN
Unexplainable

Kathleen was fidgeting with her hands as she frantically paced the hospital waiting room. She was so focused in her concern for Tyler, she didn't even realize that the sheriff was walking toward her. Tyler was her whole world and consumed most of her thoughts on any given day. The thought of anything being wrong with him, even something that most people would consider minor, seriously worried her. This accident was enough to send her into major panic-mode. And, initially, it had. The sheriff's assurance that Tyler seemed fine definitely helped, but it wasn't nearly enough. Regardless of the fact that the sheriff was someone she truly trusted, she needed a doctor's confirmation to fully calm her nerves.

She was glad the sheriff had picked her up at work and was the one to break the news of Tyler's accident to her. Their long-term friendship made it easy for her to express her bare emotions without fear of judgment and her trust in him gave his encouragement credibility. Eventually, she would get embarrassed about her reaction and apologize for her hysterics but, it would be a while before she was even aware of the way she had behaved. Not that the sheriff wouldn't understand. Of course he would. And, he did.

For now, Kathleen was barely even aware of just how thankful she was for her good friend in all of this. And, she truly was. Ron Wilson had been there for her time and again since shortly after she arrived in Penuel. They had met in the diner when Ron was a young police officer and a frequent patron. He had been there for her when Gwen died and she sometimes secretly wished she had turned to him for romantic comfort back then instead of Brett Riggle. But, then again, she wouldn't have Tyler if she had. No regrets there. Having Tyler is what caused her to throw romance out the window and focus on motherhood. She knew that Ron wanted more but she had made it clear that she wasn't offering. He still joked about the two of them dating but she had never really taken it seriously and Ron had always remained a true friend.

It can be easy to take that kind of friendship for granted at times. Or, at least, to put gratitude on a back shelf in one's heart and let other things rise to the front. Her mind, for the time being, was focused exclusively on Tyler. If life was a body of water and worry could be a substance, after all, it would be the dirt that made life murky. At this moment, her gratitude was there but it was still on that back shelf and life had become very murky that evening.

Kathleen was waiting for the sheriff to return with what he assured her would be good news in the form of her requested medical opinion. That's what she so desperately needed to calm her nerves and he understood that. Suddenly, she finally spotted the sheriff approaching and physically stopped in her tracks while her words practically lunged at him. "Ron. What'd they say?" she asked him. Waiting impatiently, she didn't get any kind of response at first. "Ron?"

The sheriff was perplexed by the entire incident. The wheels were turning as if the mouse in his brain was on performance enhancing drugs but nothing was adding up. He couldn't make sense of it. In fact, if someone had managed to capture the energy being used by both Kathleen and the sheriff's brains in that moment, they could probably power the entire town of Penuel for a solid week.

"What did they say?" Kathleen repeated eagerly.

Looking at the concerned mother in front of him, the sheriff smiled. "He's in perfect health," he finally told her, displaying much less of the enthusiasm than Kathleen responded with.

"Oh, thank God!" Kathleen exclaimed. She flailed her arms

in the air and let them land over his shoulders as she gave the sheriff a huge hug. Typically, Kathleen throwing her arms around him would have thrilled the sheriff. But, he was very distracted by the vast difference between what he knew to be normal in accidents like this and what he was actually experiencing right now.

"They both are. They cleaned 'em up. No cuts, no broken bones, not so much as a bruise."

"That's amazing."

"At least."

"What do you mean, at least?"

The sheriff's smile had faded and his perplexed look had returned. "Kathleen, I saw those cars. I saw the blood those two were covered in. I saw the clothes they were wearing that had been torn to shreds. Amazing is one way to put it but, I'm more inclined to call it impossible."

"It sounds that way but, it's obviously not impossible because it actually happened," Kathleen told him.

"Something happened. But, what exactly was it? I mean, where'd the blood come from? Kathleen, I'm telling you they have no cuts or scrapes or anything. So, I can't figure out for the life of me where that blood could have come from."

"Right now, Ron, I don't care. I just want to see my son."

"Of course," the sheriff conceded. "Come on. I'll take you

back there."

On their way to get Tyler the sheriff explained that, while Tyler was physically as fit as a fiddle, he was experiencing a certain level of shock because of the traumatic ordeal he had been through. He hadn't spoken since the accident and, while the doctors assured the sheriff that eventually he would, they couldn't guarantee any sort of a timeline for when he would start speaking again.

This news, of course, shook Kathleen up again. She hated the idea of Tyler suffering in any way and this had clearly affected his mental and emotional health. However, she was determined to appear strong for him.

When she walked in the room, she was surprised at how alert he appeared to be. The word "shocked" made her think of someone who was in a trance but Tyler was very aware of her and everything going on around him. He just seemed emotionally detached and like he had flipped a switch to turn off his talking mechanism. His eyes followed every move; he just didn't have a reaction to anything.

Kathleen doted on him. She told him how glad she was that he was okay and how much she loved him but got no response. It was disappointing but she kept her composure.

The sheriff helped Kathleen get Tyler checked out of the hospital and offered to continue to be of any assistance they needed. He didn't make it a secret that he cared very deeply for Kathleen and, by extension, Tyler. But, this was a family matter. And, no matter how much he would like the relational dynamics to be otherwise, he wasn't family.

While both the sheriff and, even more so, Kathleen were deeply concerned with Tyler's well-being, no one was more freaked out than Tyler himself. But, that's because he knew what was really going on. Well, sort of...

Who or what am I? he wondered to himself in muddled silence.

CHAPTER SIXTEEN
Control

The only light in Tyler's room was coming from two sources: the night sky outside, which peeked through the closed window blinds, and the red glow of the digital alarm clock inside, which read 3:24am. Tyler, however, was wide-awake in bed and staring at the nearly blank ceiling. The one thing the ceiling had to offer was a very faint glow from the puffy "glow in the dark" stickers in the shape of stars and planets. They had almost lost their charge now and were arranged in a pattern that not even remotely accurately resembled the universe.

Tyler had not yet slept a single wink and, as a result, he was going absolutely stir crazy. It was the first time he could remember being up so late without Preston being the cause of it. He was done with his tossing and turning, as well as his pillow shifting and blanket maneuvering. He had done as much of that as he could handle and refused to do any more. Tyler was completely still and he intended to remain that way until he fell asleep. If, in fact, he could. If he didn't, his plan was to remain in that position until daylight replaced moonlight and peeked through those window blinds.

The day's events clearly should have exhausted him to the point where a deep sleep was, not only possible but, absolutely required by both his body and his mind. Although he did feel more than a little sluggish after healing Nancy, he was somehow back to feeling normal by the time the sheriff had arrived. Now, nearly a dozen hours later, he still didn't feel the least bit tired. He added that to his mental list of the strange events of the day, which didn't exactly aid his ability to sleep either. Those strange events were the cause of the thoughts that had been keeping his mind racing all night. Unfortunately, there was no end in sight, which made his plan to lay still a complete and utter failure.

After slamming both of his fists down on the mattress at his sides, he couldn't help himself and began to review those events again. It started with not needing glasses when he woke up in the morning. That alone was completely bizarre and, on any other day, would have seemed impossible.

But, as if it weren't enough, the outlandish had continued with what he thought was called telekinetic events where he could move objects just by thinking about doing it.

Downright freaky!

Then there was the football field incident where he could suddenly see what was happening far away as if it were right in front of him. It was like he went from needing glasses to having the eyes of a hawk.

HUH?!

Then, the vision enhancement was followed by the parking lot incident where he had somehow developed Superman's ears.

WHAT?!

And, finally, he suffered a car accident that should have killed him. Yet, instead, it left him alive with the ability to heal an old woman who told him that angels had informed her he would bring her back to life. Blank. There is absolutely no reaction appropriate for that one.

It was all too weird and too crazy.

This single day contained far more strange events than anyone would ever believe could happen in an entire lifetime. And, it had left Tyler with far more questions than answers. He needed a distraction.

Tyler looked around the room and spotted his TV set. Maybe that was the distraction he was looking for. He looked around the room again, this time for the remote control, and saw it lying on his desk. He abandoned his idea of lying still when he got to his feet and walked over to it. As Tyler stretched his arm out to reach for it, it rose up into his hand. It wasn't the first time something like this had happened. In fact, it had happened several times earlier that same day. But, he hadn't gotten used to it enough to begin expecting it just yet. So, his eyes widened and then blinked a few times as he tried to process what he had just seen. *This is all so flippin' crazy!* he mentally screamed.

Walking back to his bed, Tyler turned on the TV's power. He lay down on his bed and started channel surfing. It seemed like there was nothing on but infomercials for kitchen equipment, fat loss pills, wrinkle removers, and exercise gear. *Maybe "self-improvement" really means the opposite,* he thought. *Aren't these things designed to make people feel bad about themselves so they'll buy stuff they're never going to use? Then they just end up feeling even worse. How depressing...*

Four or five minutes of that was plenty so, Tyler turned off the power on the TV. Once again, the room was mostly dark and lacking in the distraction department. *Talk about depressing,* Tyler continued his inner monologue.

Staring at the ceiling again, the boredom returned and his brain raced with random thoughts about what was happening to him. Was it a blessing, or a curse? Was he still human, an angel like the old lady thought he was, or some kind of alien freak that would soon find out his father sent him to destroy earth? *Why did Graham have to go and reference Clark Kent?* he wondered. *All I can think about is Superman comparisons. I'm no Superman. Ugh! This is all completely ridiculous!*

Seeking another distraction, he scanned the room again. This time, he rolled over and his eyes shifted down to the floor. He spotted a textbook from school and started to reach for it. Remembering the remote control, he decided to experiment. He sat up, stretched his arm out so that his hand was directly above the book, and began to concentrate. Nothing happened for a few seconds but, just before Tyler's confidence waned, the textbook suddenly wiggled a little and then shot straight up off of the ground and into his hand.

A smile crossed his face as he looked at the textbook and realized that he was beginning to take command over whatever it was that was happening to him. If he was going to read, he would need a little light. So, he stared at the light switch and concentrated as hard as he could. After a moment, the switch flipped and the light came on. Another smile crossed Tyler's face as he realized that gaining control over this could actually wind up being something useful and, even better, something he could have fun with.

He opened his book but, before he even started to read, he looked around at his messy room and recognized an opportunity to both fine-tune his new skills and be productive. He stretched his arm out again and focused on a coat that was lying on the floor next to his desk. The coat rose from the ground and followed the direction of Tyler's hand as he steered it to the closet. Tyler caused it to slide in between a couple of sweatshirts and flip each shoulder over the sides of a hanger so that it hung neatly where it belonged.

He looked around the room again. Instead of seeing a mess, he now saw a variety of prospects for skill building.

"Awesome."

CHAPTER SEVENTEEN
The First Reveal

Kathleen reluctantly left Tyler at home and went to work the morning following her son's accident. The sheriff and the doctors had assured her that it would be okay. Still, it was a difficult decision to make but she realized that they really couldn't afford for her to take a day off. With everyone telling her that Tyler would be fine, money was just too tight for her to stay.

The sheriff had offered to check in on Tyler but Kathleen decided to do that herself. So, she called home on breaks and even stopped by to share a sandwich with Tyler at lunchtime. Therefore, by the end of the workday, she had checked in five times.

She hadn't pressed Tyler on any specifics surrounding the accident or on the miracle of his survival. For now, all she really cared about was the fact that he was okay. He was. That was enough.

It was just before 4:00pm and Tyler had been sitting at the kitchen table ever since lunch with his mom. As soon as she left, he resumed the honing of his new skills. He was telekinetically moving two spoons in all different directions. Then, he moved two more spoons into the mix to create a circle and spun them for a moment before stopping them and causing them to stand on end.

A sudden knock on the door broke his concentration, causing him to divert his attention, and the spoons all collapsed onto the table. Disappointed, Tyler stood up and went to the door. He opened it and Preston burst in before an invitation could even be extended.

"Unbelievable," Preston announced.

"What?" Tyler asked as he closed the door and faced his friend.

"I just stopped by Mike's Garage and saw your truck and that lady's car," Preston explained. "Totally mangled. I can't believe you're standing here after that disaster. It's crazy. Wait." Preston paused and looked at his friend, now less amazed and even more perplexed. "Did you just talk?"

"I did," Tyler conceded sarcastically. "I've been doing that for about seventeen years now."

"I heard you were on mute."

"Maybe temporarily," Tyler conceded. "Not today."

"Good," Preston said enthusiastically before continuing with his previous topic. "Look at you."

"What?"

"You look cherry. How's that possible?"

Tyler's answer was a half-hearted *I don't know* shrug of the shoulders. The truth was, he really didn't know how it was possible. None of it made any sense to him. But, he was also hiding the fact that he knew a lot more than he was currently willing to let Preston in on. Unfortunately, for him, Preston was an equally smart and relentless guy.

"Something's going on here, man. You'd better stop playin' and drop some science on me."

Of course, Tyler knew exactly what Preston was getting at but, he didn't know if he should tell anyone what was going on with him so, he remained silent.

"I'm no gimp," Preston continued to press. "I'm your boy." Preston waited just a moment for a response but didn't get one so, again, he kept pressing. "Okay, let's dissect this. First of all, there's no way anyone could see who it was or what they were doing on that football field yesterday. That is, no one but you, apparently. And then you survive a mangler car accident without so much as a bruise or a scrape. And, the woman in the other car, who from what I hear is too old to survive a round of bumper cars that you only have to be thirty-six inches tall to participate in, she survives, too. And, again, not a single bruise or scrape on her."

"You're right," Tyler admitted. It was getting too outlandish to keep a secret from his best friend. He was beginning to cave in. "It's pretty weird."

"Not weird. Ridiculously unfeasible. Besides, you said yourself just yesterday that something unexplainable was goin' on with you. You know what it is but you're not telling your best friend. What gives, bro?"

"Preston, I don't know what's happening to me."

"But, you'll acknowledge that something is in fact happening?"

After a moment, Tyler finally nodded in agreement. "I think I have to."

"Finally."

"Something was off all day yesterday."

"No kidding," Preston deadpanned.

"I needed to come to grips with it before I talked to anyone about it. You're the first person I'm admitting this to."

"I'd better be. We're boys. Now, admit away. What exactly is it that you were coming to grips with? What's going on?"

"I'm not sure. That's the truth." Tyler paused a moment while the cave-in was completed. With the decision made, showing it off was actually going to be fun. "If I show you something," he asked, "will you promise to keep it between us?"

"Of course. I'm no ear-duster. Come on, man. It's me."

"Follow me," Tyler said as he led Preston into the living room. He opened the sliding glass door and they stepped out onto the back porch. Tyler slid the door shut and turned to face away from the house. On either side of the grass was a small pile of rocks. "I was working on this, this morning."

"Working on what?" Preston asked, confused. "I don't see anything. Are you showing me your landscaping? Because, don't tell your mom I said this but, it could use some work. I've got a sore back though so, don't ask-"

"Just watch," Tyler interrupted him as he stretched his arms out at his sides and started to slowly raise them. Two of the rocks that he was focused on, one from each pile, gradually rose into the air – following his arm movement.

Preston's mouth slowly dropped open. His eyes darted back and forth between the two rocks. He was stunned and confused. He looked at Tyler, then back at the rocks. Preston couldn't decide whether or not to believe Tyler was really causing the rocks to levitate or if he was being tricked but he was too dumbfounded to ask any questions.

Suddenly, Tyler slammed his hands together in front of him and the rocks flew across the yard and collided in the middle of it, shattering into hundreds of pieces.

"What the…? Preston asked, so freaked out he didn't finish the sentence. Then, "You'd better not be David Copperfielding me right now."

"I'm not. I promise."

"Then holy crap! What was that, dude?"

"It all started when I woke up yesterday."

"What started? You started smashing rocks without touching them?"

"Everything."

"You just woke up like this?"

"Yeah, basically."

"How?"

"Preston, I really don't know. It was just all-of-a-sudden but it was also developed gradually throughout the day. I can't explain it."

"Son-of-a…" Preston started but, once again, didn't finish his sentence as he began to pace the yard and continue freaking out. "That was awesome. I mean, that was freaking awesome!" Finally, Preston stopped and turned around to face Tyler as a devilish grin crept out of the corners of his mouth. "What else have ya got?"

CHAPTER EIGHTEEN
A Return On Deposits

Mrs. Hallowell was a regular customer of Kathleen's. She and her husband had been regular customers at the diner for breakfast every Sunday morning and she had been going to this bank for as long as Kathleen had been working there. In fact, Mrs. Hallowell had been going to this bank far longer than Kathleen had been living in Penuel.

The two of them had seen the branch go through a lot of changes over the years as the parent company was bought out by larger banks several times. It started when the locally owned Bank of Penuel, founded in 1952, was purchased in 1988 by a bank called Evergreen Mutual, which had branches across the entire state. In 1992, Evergreen Mutual was purchased by Elliot Bay Financial, which had been founded in Washington but had grown to cover the entire West Coast. Finally, in 1995, Elliot Bay Financial was purchased by a multinational banking and financial services corporation based out of North Carolina called America's Bank. In less than a decade, Kathleen had gone from working at a one-branch bank to working at one of the largest banks in the country, at branch number 4,264. With all of those changes, however, the two hardest things to get used to were driving up to a building that had been painted different colors and had a new sign with a new name and, even worse, the new computer system that had to be learned with each change. Doing the same old tasks in a new system was a real pain. But, corporate always sent someone out to do the training. Then they were gone and rarely came back to the little branch in tiny Penuel.

Over the years, Kathleen and Mrs. Hallowell had conversations with each other regarding those changes. But, far more often, their conversations were about their children and Mrs. Hallowell's grandchildren. These chats always took place at the bank's drive through window and occurred at least twice a week starting all the way back on Kathleen's very first afternoon on the job. She was about as familiar a person to Kathleen as someone who isn't a close friend or a member of the family can be.

Yet, for some reason, today, Mrs. Hallowell reminded her of Nancy Hanley for the very first time. Perhaps it was the fact that both last names started with an H. Or, maybe it was because they were both elderly women with similar family backgrounds. Mrs.

Hallowell, however, still had her ornery husband waiting for her at home. More than likely, though, it was because Kathleen hadn't stopped thinking about Tyler's accident all day, which put Nancy Hanley square at the front of her mind. *What a miracle*, she thought with a heart full of thanksgiving.

Kathleen sent the cash and receipt to Mrs. Hallowell in the outside lane through the pneumatic air tube as Sheriff Wilson drove up in the inside lane. "There you go, Mrs. Hallowell." Kathleen said. "Have a nice day. And give those grandkids an extra squeeze for me, okay?"

"Will do, dear," Mrs. Hallowell responded as she stuck her arm out of the window, reaching her hand out in anticipation of the capsule's arrival. "You do the same for that boy of yours."

"I will." Kathleen told her, meaning it more than ever – if that was even possible. "Thanks," she said with a smile before changing mental gears while she pushed a button that sent the metal drawer under the window popping out of the wall. She then flipped a lever, switching the output of the microphone in her booth to the speaker located next to the drawer. "Hi Ron," Kathleen said, greeting him with a smile.

"Hi," the sheriff responded cheerfully as he placed his check and deposit slip in the drawer. "How are you doing today, Kathleen?"

"Good. You?"

"I'm good. Thanks. How's Tyler holding up?"

"A lot better. The shock seems to be wearing off," Kathleen responded as she pressed the button again, this time closing the drawer. She took the paper items out and continued, "Although, I don't think he slept at all last night. But, at least he's talking now. Not a lot but, I'll take it."

"You bet. That's a big step in the right direction. Did he go to school today?"

"Oh, no. I didn't want him to."

"Yeah, I'm sure that's for the best. Well, if he didn't sleep last night, he'll probably sleep all day then. You have to rest at some point no matter how young and seemingly invincible you are. Especially after a major ordeal like he went through yesterday."

"True," Kathleen said as she finished the sheriff's transaction and sent him the receipt. "Sleeping all day doesn't actually sound half bad. I'd say 'Those were the days' but, the truth is, I never really had those days."

"Yeah," he responded with a chuckle. "Me neither. Teenagers grow up different nowadays than we did. But, I'd say Tyler has a pretty good excuse for a long nap right about now."

"That's for sure," Kathleen agreed. She had grown a bit more serious but her smile didn't fade as she both finished his transaction and continued the conversation. "Thanks for all of your help with Tyler, Ron. You've been really good to us."

"I have an agenda," he said as the drawer popped open again and he took his receipt.

"You do, do you?"

"Come on, Kathleen. Let's be honest with each other. You know all too well that I do. Don't you?"

"I was starting to worry that you weren't going to ask this time."

"It wouldn't be a trip to the bank if I didn't try to score a date with the teller."

"Then you're lucky I'm at the window today and not Frank."

"I've never seen Frank in a dress but, I think I can picture it and I'm inclined to agree with you."

After sharing another laugh, Kathleen conceded, albeit just a little bit, for the first time in their entire friendship. "I'll tell you what. Turn of events. Why don't you come over tonight and have dinner with Tyler and me? Give us a chance to say thank you."

"Well, that would make this the best trip to the bank I can remember. Although, it would be better if I wasn't about to drive away picturing Frank in a dress."

"Can't help you there. I'll see you around six-thirty?"

"I'll very much look forward to it."

"Me too, Ron."

With a wave, he drove away elated and Kathleen watched

him go. She felt a few flutters in her tummy as she realized how much she was looking forward to the evening. She had been good friends with Ron for what seemed like forever and they had even flirted from time to time over the years. But, she had specifically tried not to lead him on because she had not allowed herself to think about a man romantically since Tyler was born. He would be an adult soon and she had really missed feeling those little butterflies. Perhaps it was time to start allowing those thoughts to creep back in. *Better late than never,* she thought to herself.

Tyler and Preston had been arguing about what to do with Tyler's new-found abilities for over twenty minutes and Tyler was getting exasperated as he retorted, "Because Preston, I don't even know why it's happening to me or how long it will last. In fact, I don't even know what *it* is."

"Can't you see the endless possibilities in all of this?" Preston offered.

"How could I not see them? You've spent almost half an hour rattling them off. It was so extensive it sounded like you had prepared it ahead of time. But that's impossible because I know for a fact that you were unaware of what was going on with me until you came over here today. Man, you're relentless."

"I just think it would be so cool if we showed people what you-" Preston tried to squeeze in before being interrupted with an attack from Tyler.

"You saw what I can do with a couple of rocks. You tell anyone about this and you'll find out what I can do to that thing on your shoulders you call a head."

Preston stared back at Tyler for a moment before he spoke. "That was pretty lame, man."

"Too dramatic?" Tyler asked, letting his guard down.

"Just a bit," Preston told him as he made his way toward the door.

"Still, you open your mouth about this and I'll go after that melon like Gallagher packin' his Sledge-O-Matic."

"Much better."

"Think so?"

"Definitely. Love that dude. Crazy funny. Plus, one of the all-time great mustaches. We should watch some of those old videos some time. Anyway, lips are sealed, bro-Jeffe."

"Good."

"In fact," Preston proposed, "why don't we head up to the hills this weekend? We can get some bro time around a campfire and forget about all of this for a while."

"Maybe. I'll see you at school tomorrow."

Preston opened the door and reached back to bump fists with Tyler. "I'm glad you're okay, man."

Tyler raised his hand up, clinched his fist, and bumped it with his friend's. "Me too."

"I'm still trippin' out about all of this, but I'm glad you're okay."

"You're trippin'? My mind is exploding."

"You'll be fine. We'll figure it out together."

"Thanks, buddy."

"Of course. Peace."

Tyler stepped into the doorway as Preston walked out onto the porch. They quickly did their signature four-part high-five before Preston turned to go without another word.

"You guys still do that hand-shake thingy?" came a voice from the driveway.

The boys looked toward the voice as Preston stepped off the porch and spotted Jessie walking toward the house. Seeing her stirred completely different emotions in each of them. Preston immediately became annoyed while Tyler felt that same tummy flutter his mom had experienced earlier with the sheriff.

"Of course," Preston snapped in a sardonic tone. "Not everyone goes through a metamorphosis so grand as yours, Princess Butterfly. To what do we owe the honor of your presence and where, may I ask, are your royal guards?"

"Go away, Preston," Jessie fired back at him.

"Did you catch the reference there to the Princess-"

"Bride," Jessie cut him off. "Yeah, I did. Princess Buttercup. I get it. Way to go, you R.O.U.S."

"Queen of slime, filth and putrescence" Preston muttered as Jessie walked past him and approached Tyler. Finally, he stopped muttering and shouted without looking behind him. "Just don't toy with my boy. Big hearts are the easiest to break."

"What are you doing here?" Tyler asked, trying to hold back a smile while also attempting to mask his embarrassment at Preston's comment, which he and Jessie completely ignored.

"I heard about the accident," Jessie said. "Came by to see how you are."

"Okay. Come on in."

Jessie stepped inside as Tyler watched Preston shake his head in disgust and turn to leave. Tyler stepped inside and closed the door behind him.

"You want something to drink?" Tyler asked.

"No, I can't really stay very long. Graham would be pretty upset if he knew I was here."

"Right. How is my good friend, Graham?"

"Actually, he's been acting really strange since yesterday."

"Yeah?" Tyler asked, trying to dig deeper but remain subtle about it.

"Yeah, he went from mad about the whole football field thing to totally somber without any reason at all."

"Huh."

"He and a couple of his friends are being all secretive, too.

Like they don't want me or anyone else to know about something."

"That's weird."

"Very," she said before pausing to think for a moment. Finally, she made her decision. "Okay. I'm just going to ask."

"Ask what?"

"Did he have anything to do with your accident?"

Trying to hide the truth, Tyler struggled for words. "What? What do you… What do you mean?"

"Was he there when it happened?"

"Why would you think…?"

"More importantly, did he do something that might have caused it?"

Trying to hide how shocked he was by her accurate assessment of the situation, Tyler could only muster, "Jessie…"

"I just want to make sure you're not protecting him for some reason."

The statement struck a chord with Tyler. She was right. By protecting himself, he was also protecting Graham. This thought infuriated him because he had no allegiance to Graham whatsoever. In fact, he wanted nothing more than to get Graham into trouble for what he had done. So, part of Tyler wanted to spill the beans and just tell Jessie everything, but revealing the truth to too many people seemed like a really bad idea. In fact, he felt like he barely had any choice at all. He had to continue to hide it. But, a hint of truth might be the best way to do it. Therefore, he decided to run with part of the truth. Just not the part that really mattered. "I'd be the last person in all of Eastern Washington to protect Graham. I think you know that."

"I don't know," Jessie admitted.

"Think about it."

Jessie followed his advice for a minute. She still wasn't convinced but decided to let it go for now. She felt that the current status of their friendship didn't lend itself to any more pressuring. "I guess."

There was an awkward silence. Neither of them knew where to go from there. So, Tyler decided to give her a literal out. "Well, thanks for coming by."

"Oh," Jessie responded with a bit of surprise. "Okay. Yeah. Well, of course."

"I mean," Tyler started in an attempt to make sure Jessie didn't think he wanted her to leave, "you said you couldn't stay."

"Right."

"I do appreciate the visit."

"Of course. So, you're okay, then?"

"I am."

"I'm glad."

Jessie headed for the door. Tyler jumped in front of her and opened it. She stepped outside and turned back around to face him. "See you at school tomorrow?"

"You bet."

"Bye."

They exchanged a brief wave and Tyler watched her walk down the driveway and disappear up the street. The happy flutter was long gone. It had been replaced with sadness. If there was anyone he wanted to be honest with, it was Jessie. It just didn't seem possible at that point and, therefore, in a roundabout way that was completely not her fault, she had managed to break his heart once again.

CHAPTER TWENTY
Revisiting

Over the years, the distant memory of the elderly woman's visit in 1972 had surfaced in Kathleen's mind too many times to count. She often wondered who the woman was and where she came from. At first sight, she had assumed the woman was a hippie friend of her parents. That turned out, as far as she could tell, not to be the case. When she went inside the house and described the woman to her parents, they didn't know who she was talking about.

At the time, Kathleen had wondered if they were just having a little too much fun at their party. But, she brought it up again the next day and they still couldn't figure out who it was that she had encountered. She never divulged the contents of her conversation with the woman because she assumed they would think she was the one hallucinating that night. Instead, she accepted the fact that the woman would simply remain a mystery.

And, indeed she had for twenty-five years.

The woman seemed to have come from nowhere. But, she was certainly there, spoke to Kathleen, and then she was gone. Kathleen had tried to rationalize the event but it simply wasn't a rational experience. When the mysterious woman spoke to Kathleen, she knew things that Kathleen had planned to do but hadn't yet executed and hadn't even told anyone about. She had also vaguely told her about Tyler. She hadn't mentioned him by name or said precisely when he'd be born. But, she had said that Kathleen would have a son and, seven years later, she did exactly that.

A gift.

That's what the woman had called Kathleen's unborn son. She said that Kathleen would think of him as a gift. But, Kathleen always brushed that off because she figured all mothers thought of their children as gifts. If this lady was a prophet, that seemed like a pretty easy prophecy to get right. However, she hadn't mentioned any other children and that, it had turned out, was probably because Kathleen didn't end up having any other children. But, when she was younger, she had always assumed she would have a large family. Kathleen's life just hadn't turned out that way. Wanting a large family but winding up a single mother of one male child seemed like a much more difficult circumstance to correctly prophesize. Some credit had to be granted for that one.

Also, she had said that Kathleen would learn that her son was not just a gift to her but that he was actually a gift to everyone. That made it sound like her son had some grand purpose. Of course, to believe that, you'd have to believe that the woman wasn't a quack. She had gotten everything right so far. But, it was still really hard to believe. And, his being a gift to everyone seemed a little far-fetched to Kathleen at this point.

Tyler was just Tyler. He was a teenager. He was a great kid and he was special to Kathleen but she couldn't imagine that he seemed extraordinary from an outsider's perspective. He wasn't an all-American athlete or a brilliant concert pianist. Tyler got good grades but he wasn't exactly at the top of his class. He wasn't some dazzling orator, artist, or science wiz-kid. Kathleen loved him more than anything in her life and he was absolutely an undisputable gift to her but, so far, she didn't see how he was a gift to the masses. Then again, he was merely seventeen years old. Only time would tell.

It had been a while since these thoughts had surfaced but they would soon come flooding back. And, they would be bringing with them all new surprises.

Kathleen was jovial as she picked her tomatoes, placed them in a plastic bag, spun the top of the bag to close it up, and put it in her cart next to her red onion, garlic cloves and fresh basil. She then pushed her cart out of the produce section and turned a corner to go down the next aisle where she planned to grab a box of spaghetti noodles before heading out in search of a decent, albeit inexpensive, bottle of red wine.

However, as she looked down the aisle, she saw something that stopped her right there in her tracks. Standing still with her shoulders squared toward Kathleen, seemingly in wait at the opposite end of the aisle, was the elderly woman who had appeared in Kathleen's parents' driveway twenty-five years earlier. Her hair and clothing had been updated with the times from the long straight hair and outrageous hippie garb to a more minimalist-inspired professional hairstyle and beige pantsuit. But, otherwise, she looked exactly the same. She didn't appear to have aged a single day in two and a half decades. Had Kathleen not been so utterly shocked to her core, she probably would have wondered how in the world that could be. Instead, she instantly recognized her but had trouble processing the reality of the situation. The resulting shockwave hit her body and froze her where she stood like the proverbial deer in the headlights.

The woman's lips didn't move. She and Kathleen were standing at opposite ends of the aisle, but her voice seemed to whisper in Kathleen's ear, "It's good to see you well, Flower. You've grown into the woman you were meant to be. Now, Tyler will become the man he was meant to be. I'm sure that, by now, you realize the revelation of the gift has begun."

Coupled with Tyler's accident just the day before and the sheriff's word, *impossible*, Kathleen's thoughts and emotions were immediately flooded with the replaying of the woman's twenty-five year-old prophecy. She replayed it repeatedly like a sportscaster might do for a great play in a nationally televised football game. Terrified, Kathleen began running toward the woman, pushing her cart in front of her.

The elderly woman slowly turned to her right and walked casually out of view. Kathleen was frantic by the time she reached the end of the aisle. She nearly ran into another customer like kids playing bumper cars and, after a very swift apology, discovered that the mysterious woman had vanished the same way she did the first time they met.

Kathleen searched in front of her but the woman was gone. She let go of the cart and rushed to look down the next aisle but there was no sign of the enigmatic, old but somehow ageless, woman. Kathleen kept walking. She searched the next aisle and then the one after that. She looked everywhere but the woman was just flat out gone. This was getting to be an incredibly frustrating pattern. Twice now, this woman had appeared, said something creepy and then disappeared with no explanation. But, for Kathleen, at this moment, the feeling of frustration quickly turned to one of terror.

Leaving her shopping cart where it was, Kathleen forgot all about her dinner plans and pretty much everything else as she sprinted out of the store to go and find Tyler.

CHAPTER TWENTY-ONE
The Second Reveal

Speeding toward the house in her brown 1985 Buick Regal, Kathleen's mind was sprinting like an Olympic track star on the final leg of an eight hundred meter race. She briefly considered the humorous possibility of getting pulled over for speeding by the sheriff and then imagined giving him the ten-second version of what had happened. The brief daydream ended with Ron giving her a police escort home – lights, siren: the whole shebang. Of course, none of that ever happened and the thought was quickly pushed out of her mind by the montage of past, present and future thoughts about Tyler.

She wondered what had been going on with Tyler that he hadn't told her about and how long it had been happening. She wondered what he must be going through right now and how, by not sharing it with her, he must feel all alone and probably terrified. And, she wondered what the future would hold for the both of them. *Please, Father, don't let me lose my son,* she prayed. Kathleen had prayed more in the last twenty-four hours than she had in the previous twenty-four days combined and all of it had been about Tyler.

With one hand pressing the button on the garage door opener, Kathleen whipped around the corner and into the driveway with the garage door already half open. She let go of the opener and pulled straight into the garage, nearly scraping the roof of her car on the bottom of the still rising door. She turned the car off and rushed into the house, forgetting both her purse and the usual step of closing the garage door.

Kathleen speed-walked through the living room, the kitchen, down the hallway to Tyler's room, and barged in without knocking.

"Mom," Tyler said, quickly irritated. "You didn't knock. You're supposed to-"

"You're going to tell me what's going on," Kathleen announced, completely interrupting Tyler and ignoring his complaint.

"Slow down, scary version of my mom. Going on with what exactly?"

"With what?" Kathleen asked, thinking it was pretty obvious.

"I'd appreciate it if you were a little more specific. You left things pretty much wide open."

"You want specifics?"

"Well, yeah. That would help me out a lot. It's why I asked for them."

"How's this for specific? I want to know how you survived that car accident."

"Oh," Tyler discerned out loud.

"And, I want to know how Nancy Hanley survived that car accident. I want to know how you both got out of your completely demolished cars without a single mark on your bodies. And, if neither of you were ever hurt, where'd all of the blood Sheriff Wilson told me about come from? I want some answers and I want them right now."

"Okay."

"Okay?"

"I said okay, mom."

"Thank you. And, thank you for finally cleaning your room, by the way. I don't think I've ever seen it look this nice. Now, get started. And, while we're at it, you really aren't wearing contacts, are you?"

Silence.

"Are you?"

"Have you finished bombarding me?"

"Hardly."

"If you want me to answer then it's going to have to be my

turn to talk. Geez. You're like a fifty year-old talking kitten."

"Forty-three."

"Close enough."

"Not for me, it isn't. Now, start talking."

"Well actually, instead of talking, how about I show you how I cleaned my room?"

"I really don't see how that-"

"Just trust me," Tyler interrupted her as he stretched his right arm forward and opened his hand toward his closet.

"What are you…" Kathleen started to say as she turned to look at the closet to see what it was Tyler was reaching toward. She watched as a wire hanger, holding a jacket, lifted off of the wooden rod that all of the clothes hung on. Her mouth slowly opened and her eyes grew wider as she watched the coat and hanger float toward her son. It stopped just above his left hand, which Tyler turned palm upward and bent his pinky and ring finger in. The hanger finally settled on Tyler's outstretched middle and index fingers.

Tyler telekinetically unzipped his coat with his right hand and floated it off of the hanger and over to his chair where it gently collapsed over the back. He then grabbed the hanger with his right hand and pressed the end of the wire hanger's hook into the palm of his left hand, causing it to bleed.

"Tyler!" Kathleen shouted as she watched the blood spill out and puddle in his palm. Instead of pulling it out, he made the cut worse by sliding the metal hook across his palm, creating a long and deep incision. "What are you doing?"

"Follow me," Tyler said as he walked past her and into the bathroom.

She followed him and watched as he calmly set the hanger on the counter and turned the water on in the sink. He rinsed the blood out of his hand and held it out for her to see. Not only was there no longer a cut there but, she saw the end of the healing process as the new scar tissue turned from pink into Tyler's natural skin color and blend in completely so there was no evidence of a cut having ever been there. "What?" Kathleen questioned. "How?"

"Now," Tyler said, "give me your hand."

Tyler reached for his mom's hand but she yanked it away.

"No," she said emphatically. "I believe you. There is no need to cut me to prove your point. I watched what you did. You're not doing it to me."

"Fair enough."

"Okay, then. Just give me a minute to process this."

"Take as many as you need. It took me all of last night."

Kathleen briefly considered what all of this meant. Finally, she spoke. "So, you healed yourself and Nancy Hanley, too."

Tyler nodded in agreement.

"I can't believe this is happening. I can't believe she was right."

"Who?" Tyler probed excitedly. "Who was right?"

"The old woman in my parents' driveway."

"Excuse me?"

"Twenty-five years ago, this woman told me that I'd have a son someday who I would eventually realize was a gift not only to me, but to everyone."

"You knew this was coming and you didn't warn me?"

"Tyler, I didn't know what she meant. Besides, I didn't believe it. I thought she was one of your grandparents' old hippie friends, stoned out of her mind. Why would I believe her?"

"You believe her now?"

"Don't really have a choice, do I? This has to stay between us, Tyler."

As he was about to reply, Tyler realized he'd already told someone. "And Preston," he admitted.

"You told Preston?"

"He's my best friend, mom."

"I don't care what he is. He's got a bigger mouth than Mick Jagger," Kathleen told her son and then promptly chuckled at her own joke.

Tyler looked at her in a way that informed her that he didn't think it was as funny as she did. "Don't worry about it," he responded.

"I am worried about it. It's Preston for crying out loud."

"Too late."

Suddenly realizing the order of things, Kathleen exclaimed, "You told Preston before me?"

"Only by a couple of hours, Mom. You were at work. It's over. Moving on…"

"Fine. Just make sure he keeps that big mouth shut."

"He's been warned."

"With death or worse, I hope"

"Close enough."

"Good," Kathleen said as she began to study Tyler's face. "You're really not wearing contacts, are you?"

<u>CHAPTER TWENTY-TWO</u>
Leftovers

"I know there's nothing we can do about the fact that Preston knows what's going on with you," Kathleen persisted as she and Tyler meandered out of his room and down the hallway toward the kitchen. "But, it's critical that no one else knows until we can figure out what it is that's going on. I mean it. No one."

"Who else do you think I'm going to tell?" Tyler asked as if he was responding to the most insane statement he'd ever heard. "I totally agree with you. Trust me. You don't have to worry about me telling anyone else. I swear. There's probably no one that would want this public less than I do."

"Good," Kathleen said as she placed an arm around her son's back and kissed his cheek. "I just want to keep you safe."

"Once again, we're on the same page. And, Preston doesn't know everything. Obviously. Because until you got home a little bit ago, there was a whole lot I didn't know."

"Fair," Kathleen acknowledged. "Now you know everything I know."

"And, vice-versa."

"Good," she said again as she kissed his cheek one more time.

An unexpected knock at the front door startled both of them as they turned toward the noise like they would if they had just finished watching a scary movie. An irrational fear washed over each of them as they silently wondered who it was at the door. Reflections on old movies and TV shows where government agents showed up at people's front doors and aliens were studied in labs flooded their minds.

The fears quickly settled as logical thoughts returned and pushed the illogical ones out.

Then…

Kathleen abruptly panicked as she remembered who was likely to be at the door, "Oh, no."

"It's just a knock," Tyler tried to reassure her. "Maybe it's Preston again. Or…"

"What time is it?" Kathleen injected into the conversation.

"About six-thirty," Tyler said with curiosity in his voice. "Why?"

"Oh, no, no, no."

"What?"

"How is it that late already?"

"Do you need me to explain to you how time works?" Tyler asked with a grin on his face that would make a Nobel Prize laureate feel stupid. Then, moving on… "Are you expecting someone?"

"I have to fix dinner," Kathleen said hurrying into the kitchen. "Answer the door, Smarty-Pants."

"Who is it?"

"Ron."

"Ron Wilson?" Tyler asked as he followed her. "The sheriff? You finally agreed to a date?"

"It's not a date."

"Oh, it's a date. But, why tonight?"

"Just… Just answer the door!"

"Alright, alright," Tyler said, heading for the front door as a second knock sounded and his mom scrambled into the kitchen. He opened the door and greeted the sheriff casually. "Hi, Sheriff."

"There he is," the sheriff announced. "Glad to hear you got your words back."

"Me, too."

"I think it's understandable you needed some time to process everything that happened. What a day, huh?"

"Yeah," Tyler agreed while withholding the *You have no idea* comment that he wanted to add on. "I guess so. Come on in."

The sheriff walked inside and Tyler shut the door behind him. "Your garage door is open, by the way."

"It is?" Tyler asked as he started off toward the back of the house. "My mom must've forgotten it. I'll get it."

"She was probably just in a hurry to check on her boy. Speaking of your mom, the cook busy in the kitchen?" the sheriff asked Tyler as he left the room, loud enough for Kathleen to hear, while attempting to hide the fact that he had already noticed the lack of food smell in the air.

"Very!" Tyler shouted as he entered the garage and reached for the button on the wall to shut the door.

Suddenly, Kathleen poked her head out of the kitchen to add her own answer to the question. "I'm a little embarrassed to admit that I ran out of time to get groceries and I'm just getting started."

"No problem," the sheriff said as he heard the garage door start to close. "Tyler can keep me company while you figure it out. Unless you want some help. I'm not all that great in the kitchen but, I could lend an extra set of hands."

"I didn't ask you over here to put you to work. You relax. I'll pour some waters. I meant to get wine but like I said…"

"You ran out of time. Water sounds great."

"How hungry are you?" Kathleen asked as she disappeared

back into the kitchen to pour the waters.

"I told you I'd bring my appetite."

"Well, we have two options."

"Okay."

"I can do oven-roasted pork with potatoes, carrots and onions but dinner will be served around eight o'clock. Or, I can re-heat last night's chicken tetrazzini and whip up a salad. That'll put dinner on the table in about twenty minutes."

"Last night's chicken whatever you said that sounded like the name of an old-timey magician would be great if you guys are okay with having it two nights in a row."

"I'm pretty sure yours is the only vote that matters in this situation, Sheriff," Tyler chimed in as he re-entered the room.

"Chicken Tetrazzini it is," Kathleen announced as she reappeared from the kitchen with two glasses of water. "Here you are."

"Thank you," the sheriff said as he took his glass.

"Thanks," Tyler added, taking his.

"You bet," Kathleen acknowledged. "See you in twenty minutes," she added as she disappeared again.

"And off she goes," the sheriff said with a chuckle as he turned his attention back to Tyler.

"To work her magic," Tyler agreed as he offered his glass to the sheriff for a cheerful clink. "To The Great Tetrazzini."

The sheriff's chuckle turned into a full-on laugh in response to Tyler's clever wit as he clinked his glass against Tyler's. As the laughter settled, the sheriff turned the topic of conversation into a segue: "You know, I hate to mix business with pleasure but, speaking of magical events, I am going to need you to come down to the cop shop and answer a few questions about the accident. When you're ready, of course."

This not only unsettled Tyler a bit, but it also perked Kathleen's listening ears in the kitchen. She had just been telling Tyler to keep this whole situation to himself and now her dinner guest was asking him to talk about it. This wasn't the sheriff's fault and was actually to be expected. It just came with a certain sense of uneasiness for both Tyler and Kathleen.

"How soon?" Tyler asked, doing his best to hide the increasing nervousness he felt.

"Like I said, when you're ready. Just, whenever you can. I don't want to make a big deal out of it. I just have to get the report filed in the next couple of days. And, I need to get your take on things to do that."

"Fair enough. After school okay?"

"You bet."

"I'll be there in the next couple of days."

"Perfect," the sheriff told him as he pulled his wallet out and dug up a business card to hand to Tyler. "Just call first so I can make sure I'm around. I'll even pick you up if you need a ride."

"My friend Preston can probably take me but I'll let you know."

"Sounds good," the sheriff agreed. Sensing a bit of apprehension, but not knowing exactly why, the sheriff decided to try and reassure Tyler: "It won't take long. It's more of a formality than anything. I had to do the same with Nancy today."

"How'd that go?"

With another chuckle, the sheriff responded: "Oh, she still thinks you're some kind of an angel in the flesh."

CHAPTER TWENTY-THREE

Clean-Up

The nerves quickly settled as the sheriff and Tyler shifted the conversation from the accident to music. Ron was proud to inform Tyler that the grunge bands he loved weren't the only Seattleites to make it big on the music scene. There was an amazing heritage to be proud of that went back a long way – even before Sub Pop Records.

He started out mentioning the heavy metal band Queensryche from the eighties. Tyler was familiar with them from their top ten hit *Silent Lucidity* that had landed on the radio around the same time Tyler originally started paying attention to new music at the age of ten. The sheriff then harkened back to other big named musicians from his own heyday like Jimi Hendrix, with whom Tyler first became familiar because of the *Foxy Lady* scene in the movie *Wayne's World*, and Merrilee Rush, who Tyler also knew because his mom considered the song *Angel of the Morning* one of her all-time favorites. The sheriff also noted that some great musicians who were not originally from the area got their start in Seattle, including Quincy Jones and Ray Charles.

Each of them having a love for music, particularly a pride in music that started in Washington State, gave them an instant connection. It wasn't that they didn't already know each other. They had known each other on some level for all of Tyler's life. But, this was a conversation they had never had before and the common ground strengthened their bond in a way both of them silently appreciated.

It was a conversation that probably could have lasted for at least another hour. But, true to her word, Kathleen was serving dinner in just under twenty minutes. She enjoyed listening to her son and the sheriff talk, but she was also excited to join the fun. And, when she did, Ron was very complimentary about the leftover chicken tetrazzini. He was not shy about allowing Kathleen to understand he hoped for another get-together in the very near future. Subtlety, at least when it came to Kathleen, was a completely foreign concept to the sheriff. And, Tyler enjoyed seeing his mom receive a heavy load of appreciation because he knew she deserved it.

The camaraderie amongst the three of them was remarkably easy, even natural. That comfort was greatly aided by the two decades of friendship between Ron and Kathleen that preceded any notion of romance, at least on Kathleen's part. There was never a prolonged lull in the conversation during the whole evening and the subject of the accident was barely touched upon other than a little water-glass toast by the sheriff over Tyler's miraculous survival.

When dinner was finished, Tyler placed his dishes in the sink, said he had homework to do, and left his mom and Ron to chat. He closed his door and lay down on his bed. He could hear them talking and laughing but abstained from taking advantage of his newly enhanced hearing abilities to eavesdrop. Instead, he decided to play a video game. As he was pulling *Tomb Raider* out of its case, he wondered why he hadn't thought of playing a video game when he couldn't sleep the night before.

Tyler eventually heard the front door close, correctly assumed the sheriff had left as happy as a little boy on Christmas morning, hit pause on *Tomb Raider* and popped off of his bed to go find out what his far-more-difficult-to-read mom was thinking about the evening. He opened his bedroom door and walked down the hallway to the kitchen where he found his mom clearing what little remained on the table.

"So…" he hinted as he turned the water on in the sink and started rinsing the dishes before placing them in the dishwasher.

"So, what?" Kathleen responded demurely.

"What were you two talking about all night?"

"It was hardly all night, Tyler. It was barely a couple of

hours."

"And?"

"And, what?"

"And, what were you talking about for those couple of hours?"

"Nothing. Everything."

"Man, can you ever paint a picture with words," Tyler said, sarcastically.

"What are you looking for?"

"Something less Jackson Pollock and more Bob Ross."

"Cute. I mean, what do you want me to say?" Kathleen asked, defiantly.

"I just want to know how it went and where it's going."

"It was just a home cooked meal to say thank you for his recent kindness."

"Not helpful because it's not new information. How about this? Are you going out again?"

"What do you mean, again? I heated up leftovers at home with my son and an old friend. This was hardly going out."

"Are you going to, for the very first time, see each other socially without having declared a not-to-be-crossed border of friendship?" Tyler asked his mom, growing increasingly impatient with her pattern of purposely avoiding answering his questions.

"I think so," Kathleen finally admitted, stopping to think

about it for a moment before picking up the salt and pepper shakers and carrying them over to the cupboard.

"Nice work, Mom. That's called conversational progress."

"Would you be okay with that?"

"Conversational progress? Yeah, right now I'm actually thinking that I'd like to see a lot more of it and prefer that it also happen a lot more frequently, if you want to know the truth."

"You know what I mean, Smart-Alec. Would you be okay with us seeing each other?"

"Romantically?"

"Yes," Kathleen said, surprising herself by once again finally admitting something for the very first time. "Romantically."

"I'd be more than okay with it. I'd be in favor of it. I'm pretty sure it's been about eighteen years since you've seen any action. That's a long drought for an adult woman."

"Tyler!" Kathleen shouted, both embarrassed and appalled at his brazen statement.

"You know what I'm saying."

"I'm not sure I do. What do you know about *seeing action*, anyway?"

"Not much. Still waiting on round one."

"Good."

"But, am I wrong?"

"Go do your homework."

"It's done."

"Well, go do something," Kathleen told him, playfully. "Stop bugging me."

"Why would I stop? It's way too much fun."

"Fun for you, maybe. I'm so glad you can get a laugh at my expense. Really. You're welcome for that."

"Thank you so much… In all seriousness, I just think it would be great to see you with a guy, and Sheriff Wilson seems like a good one. That's all."

"Well, I agree with you and that's all fine and dandy, but I'd rather not talk with my son about *seeing action*."

"That's fair."

"Well, thank *you* so much," Kathleen repeated back to her son with a heavy layer of playful mockery.

"You're welcome so very much. Now, go get some," Tyler said as he flicked her in the face with water from his wet hands.

"What is the matter with you tonight?" Kathleen shouted, laughing, as she rushed over and splashed him with a cupped hand full of water directly from the sink.

Everything seemed back to normal for the moment. Improved, even, with the addition of the new role Sheriff Wilson was beginning to take on in their lives. Unfortunately for all three of them, it was only a temporary reprieve as more trouble was lurking just around the proverbial bend.

CHAPTER TWENTY-FOUR
Pep

Tyler opened the door to Preston's Fuego and immediately greeted his friend. "Mornin'."

"Mornin' Glory, did you see the reindeer?" Preston asked in a voice that sounded like a crazy morning radio personality.

As the two of them grabbed everything from empty Gatorade bottles to bags from fast food restaurants and tossed them into the back seat to make room for Tyler in the front, Tyler also glanced around but saw no reindeer. "What?" Tyler asked, genuinely confused.

"Nothin'," Preston said before going on to explain himself. "It's just something lame my dad says whenever he wakes me up.

"Where is it from and what does it mean?" Tyler asked, completely perplexed, as he finally sat down and closed the door behind him.

"I have no idea. Apparently, his dad used to say it to him and

I'm totally going to harass my kid with it someday, too." Preston hit the gas and pulled away from Tyler's house.

"Why?"

"For fun. And, now it's a family tradition so, I totally have to carry it on."

"Even though you don't know what it means."

"Yep. That's the rule."

"Okay," Tyler said, letting it go.

"So, was your mom all smiles this morning?"

"She was in an extra good mood. For sure."

"It's so gross thinking about old people getting all romantic."

"She's not that old. She's forty-three."

"Old enough. And, she's your mom. That's gross."

"Aren't you the guy that was talking about how hot Jessie's mom is?"

"That's different."

"Not remotely."

"It's totally different."

"How?"

"It's not your mom."

"It's Jessie's mom."

"Exactly. Totally different."

"You make no sense."

"I make perfect sense. You shouldn't think your mom is hot

but I can think Jessie's mom is hot."

"I always knew you were a few bulbs short of a Lite Brite set but you're even starting to scare me. She's more than twice your age, dude."

"Fine wine."

"We've been over this. You wouldn't be able to tell the difference between fine wine and red wine vinaigrette."

"You know what I mean."

"I know what you mean and it's messed up."

"So, you're going to stick to your guns and tell me it's super-sized gross for me to think Jessie's mom is hot but you're totally cool thinking about your mom getting all smoochy-woochy with Sheriff Wilson? Because, to me, that's messed up in the most Freudian of ways."

"Well, I don't want to think about it, no. I just want her to be happy, ya weirdo. Can we change the subject? Or, put on some music or something? I really need to black out the images you've placed in my head."

"Fine," Preston agreed as he reached forward and turned on the radio. It cut in, in the middle of the song *Just a Girl* by No Doubt and the conversation quickly ended as the head-bobbing to the beat of the music, coupled with a bit of mumbled singing, began.

By the time they arrived at the school the music coming from the radio had transitioned to *Bullet With Butterfly Wings* by The Smashing Pumpkins. As they pulled into the parking lot, Tyler could see and feel people looking at him and talking. They peered in the car windows from a distance, sometimes even pointing at him, and making comments to friends. Billy Corgan's voice emanated from the radio, singing about being a rat in a cage.

"This song suddenly feels very appropriate," Tyler acknowledged to his friend.

"Yeah," Preston agreed as he parked the car and turned the engine off. "Kind of creepy."

"Not kind of."

"Well, you could always embrace the fame."

"No thanks."

Some people, like Preston and Graham, are born with a desire to be out in front of the pack and get noticed. Other people, like Tyler, prefer to fly under the radar. This had the makings of an incredibly uncomfortable situation for a guy like Tyler and his stress level was quickly rising.

"I'm not so sure you have a choice in the matter at this point."

"I could go back home."

"You have to face it at some point."

"True."

"Ready?" Preston asked, sensing Tyler's anxiety as he

gripped the door handle.

"Not really," Tyler answered, honestly. "I don't like being on display."

"I'm telling you - embrace it," Preston instructed Tyler. "If you're going to be on display, at least it's more trophy case and less basket case. You're a walking miracle. Everyone loves a miracle."

"I'd rather they just left me alone. I feel less like a miracle and more like a spectacle."

"This'll be good for you, man. You'll see. Popularity has its advantages. Ladies in spades, for one. Come on, bro. Let's do this."

Preston and Tyler finally opened their doors and stepped out of the car. They locked and shut the doors behind them and started walking toward the school. Suddenly, Preston noticed that Tyler didn't have his usual backpack full of books.

"Where's your stuff?" Preston asked.

"I don't need it," Tyler answered.

"What about your books? You finally packin' light like your main man, Preston?"

"Yeah, I guess so."

"What changed?"

Tyler flashed Preston a *Duh, everything changed* look. "I just don't need them."

Preston mocked Tyler by flashing him with a look of his own. This one said *I'm waiting for more information.*

"I read them already," Tyler finally admitted. "Memorized them, actually."

"Seriously? All of them?"

"Yep."

"That's crazy," Preston stated as he looked around and started noticing that a lot of people seemed to be walking out of the main building instead of into it. "At least I know who to cheat off of."

"Not happening," Tyler stated halfheartedly because he was distracted by the same thing Preston was. Finally, he asked the question on both of their minds, "Where's everyone going?"

"I don't know," Preston responded before stopping one of the oncoming students. "Hey, where're you bookin' to?"

"Morning pep-assembly," the student answered. "I guess they're going to make some big announcement."

Preston looked at Tyler as the student walked away. Tyler was visibly worried. He couldn't help but speculate on the possibility of this having something to do with him.

Is the faculty going to make a big deal about the survival of the accident and draw even more attention to me? he wondered. *What a nightmare. Only one way to find out what's going on,* he decided as his anxiety level spiked.

Preston tried to play it off, "Lame!" he announced. "To the gym?"

"To the gym," Tyler reluctantly agreed.

"I got no pep for this stupid school," Preston joked.

"What does pep even mean, anyway?"

"No clue."

So, off to the gym they went without the slightest idea just how pinnacle of a moment this assembly would be for Tyler and even less awareness of exactly how or why it would prove to be so important.

CHAPTER TWENTY-FIVE
Assembly

Preston led Tyler into the high school gymnasium and passed a bunch of crowded bleachers, looking for a place for the two of them to sit. Tyler mostly stared at the floor in front of him as they walked but he could still sense the many students pointing at him. Although he avoided using his hearing ability, he heard his name mentioned over and over again as students talked about the accident. The feeling of being a caged animal on display was showing no signs of diminishing.

"Is this ever going to go away?" he wondered out loud.

"You've only been back for like five minutes," Preston told him. "What do you expect? It just started. This is only the beginning. It's not going anywhere any time soon. I'm telling you, bro, you'll be a lot better off if you find a way to enjoy it. Embrace the fleeting celebrity while you still can. Revel in your moment before it's gone."

"Right," Tyler said sarcastically even though he knew there was some truth to what Preston was telling him. He just wasn't built to enjoy this kind of attention.

Preston turned left and stepped up into the bleachers. Tyler followed him as they worked their way to the top and stepped in front of some other students to claim their empty stretch of pine. Preston immediately pulled a Ziplock baggy full of crushed potato chips out of his pocket, opened it up, and started eating.

Noticing this, Tyler asked, "What is that? Potato chips? At eight o'clock in the morning?"

"Breakfast," Preston responded, casually.

"Nice," Tyler said with a chuckle. "Breakfast of champions."

"Exactly. I'm in training."

"Yeah? For what?"

"Math Olympics."

"You're no mathlete. In fact, you suck at math."

"That's why I'm in training. When I work this bag back to zero, my training will be complete."

"Who's your trainer?"

"Johnny Ruffle. And, don't question his methods."

"I wouldn't dare," Tyler insisted as they both laughed. Tyler's smile slowly faded as he looked at the wall behind the basketball hoop on his left. He studied the banners. Penuel High School had obviously had some good men's basketball teams in the seventies and girls' volleyball teams in the eighties. But, the nineties had been all about football. The football banner already listed three State Championships for that decade, including each of the last two seasons.

Within just a few seconds, an onslaught of thoughts intersected inside of Tyler's mind. They started with the thought that he really hadn't been a part of anything significant while in school. He quickly scanned his memories of the elementary years. Then junior high. Finally, the last four years at Penuel High School. He couldn't think of a single thing he had done that people would remember. Certainly, nothing that would be celebrated years later the way those athletic achievements on the wall would be. It was a lonely feeling.

He briefly wondered if Preston was right. Preston had a point when he said he'd be better off accepting the fact that people were excited about him surviving that car accident. The quandary was, how could he separate that from the miracle happening to him, which he also knew he shouldn't make public?

But, none of that was really the point. The thought that really made Tyler's skin begin to crawl was when he started to wonder why those legacies, the accomplishments that people still took pride in decades later, were reserved for jerks like Graham. *Maybe nice guys really do finish last,* he thought as the anger stirred inside of him.

It was right about that time that Coach Clark stepped in front of the microphone in the middle of the basketball court. He was drinking a cup of coffee from the teacher's lounge that most of the teachers had learned to stay away from and had nicknamed *the sludge*. As he began to speak, the crowd quieted down but Tyler's thoughts, and particularly his anger, were increasing considerably.

"You know," Coach Clark began, "once in a while, a special athlete comes along who fulfills his coach's dreams. The coach recognizes the athlete's talents and hopes that he can help him to become everything he can be. If he is really lucky, that athlete actually does it. I've been blessed with one such athlete and have had the pleasure of working with him over the last four years."

You have got to be kidding me, Tyler thought to himself as he and Preston looked at each other and they simultaneously said what the coach hadn't yet, "Graham."

Tyler should have concentrated on the feeling of relief that came from discovering this event had nothing to do with him. Instead, the anger and frustration had been fomenting and it finally reached the boiling point at the thought of Graham being honored after turning Tyler's life upside down.

"I'm not the only one who has recognized this," Coach Clark resumed.

As if reading Tyler's mind, Preston got a twinkle in his eye.

He leaned over and whispered to Tyler like a devil on his shoulder, "I'm thinking this would be a great time for revenge."

"The Seattle Times," the coach continued, "has announced their pick for Washington State's Athlete of the Year."

The crowd began to applaud and Tyler's emotions hit their zenith. "I agree," Tyler whispered back to Preston.

Tyler didn't see Preston give him a look that showed his pleasant surprise at Tyler's response.

"Any guesses on who they picked?" Coach Clark proposed.

The crowd started shouting variations on Graham's name like *Zimmerman, Zimmy*, and *The Zim-Man*.

"That's right," Coach Clark announced. "Our very own, Graham Zimmerman."

Graham stood up with both hands raised, waving to the crowd like a celebrity on the red carpet at a big movie premier or an awards show. He walked out to the microphone and faced his audience, continuing to wave with both of his hands still in the air. "Thanks, everybody. These four years have been awesome. I just wish I could stay here one more year and bring this school another State title."

As if you're the only player on the team, you cocky jerk, Tyler thought to himself.

"But," Graham continued, "if you want to see me play next year, it won't be too long of a drive. Just head east a couple of hours until you hit Pullman where I'll be playing for the Cougars!"

"That's it," Tyler said quietly as the crowd cheered wildly for Graham. "Fun's over for you, Zim-Man. But, it's just getting started for me." Tyler couldn't take anymore. His rage was finally uncontainable.

Suddenly, Graham's pants unzipped, the button popped out, his belt unbuckled, and his pants dropped to his ankles. He suddenly found himself standing in front of the entire student body and faculty in his boxer shorts.

"What the…?" Graham wondered out loud into the microphone as he looked down at his bare legs and bent over to lift his jeans back up from his ankles. Suddenly, while everyone was watching and laughing hysterically, Coach Clark's coffee flew out of his hand and exploded over Graham's crotch. Graham fell immediately to the floor, with his jeans around his knees, and screamed in pain.

Preston looked at Tyler, with a mouth full of chips, and said in casual amazement, "You're the devil."

"I may be. I don't know what I am anymore."

CHAPTER TWENTY-SIX
Remorse

Tyler was feeling a tremendous amount of relief. Having been to several classes that morning, it was clear that everyone had essentially moved on from the instantly old news of his and the old lady's miraculous survival in the horrific car-accident. They were now focused on the most recent astounding event – Graham's nearly naked, magnetic coffee dance. Thankfully, no one besides Preston knew that this second event also involved Tyler.

Furthermore, Tyler thought, it seemed appropriate to have the spotlight on the person who was responsible for his accident in the first place. If people had known Graham was the one who caused the car accident, they would be talking about him anyway. So, the attention was now where it clearly belonged. As far as Tyler was concerned, whether it was for the right reason or not seemed a little beside the point. All he had done was to set things right. He was the innocent victim, after all. Why should he have to also endure all of that attention that he dreaded so much? Even more, it felt like sweet revenge to have that spotlight on something so humiliating. After all, a jerk like Graham deserved that kind of notoriety instead of the overrated glory that his athletic abilities were earning for him.

Tyler was at his locker in a hallway crowded with students. Most of whom were, of course, still talking about the crazy morning pep assembly. Some were even re-enacting Graham's fiasco and laughing uproariously about it. Those were the students that painted an irresistible devilish grin on Tyler's face. Others, on the other hand, were expressing deep concern and sympathy over Graham's state of being.

Could Graham wind up getting empathy instead of ridicule for this, Tyler suddenly wondered. That outcome might very well have been his new worst nightmare. But Tyler ultimately brushed it off. *Nah, nobody is that lucky.*

At this point in the day, Tyler would typically be placing his books in his locker. Since he no longer needed them, today he simply pulled his sack lunch out and closed the door. After pushing the shackle back into the body of the padlock and turning the dial to lock it, Tyler spun around and immediately noticed Jessie slowly approaching from down the hall. Unfortunately, she didn't seem to notice him. She had her books pulled in to her chest and looked zoned out, like the most beautiful zombie to ever walk the halls of any high school anywhere.

Maybe it was the good feeling about the shift in student-body conversation. Perhaps it was the control he'd taken over his new abilities. Or, it could simply be the fact that she had stopped by his house yesterday and it felt like a new chapter in their relationship had been opened. Whatever it was, for once, his desire to try talking to her finally overcame his unrelenting nerves.

"Hey," Tyler said, announcing his presence. His voice startled Jessie who looked concerned about something. "You okay?" he asked her.

"Oh," Jessie started in response. "Uh, yeah. Yeah, I'm fine. Of course."

"You sure?"

"Yeah, yeah. Fine. Really." She had to hit the mental pause button for a second in order to let her brain try to catch up and be present in the moment. Finally, "Boy, things are kind of weird around here lately though, huh?"

"You mean the assembly?"

"Yeah, that and your accident," Jessie said, still in kind of a ponderous state. "Everything just seems, I don't know, strange. Like, borderline paranormal. Twilight Zone-ish. You know what I mean?"

"I guess so," Tyler admitted sheepishly. "Yeah."

"I'm sure that sounds totally crazy," she admitted, as a self-defense mechanism, before he could say anything to make her feel like she had lost her mind. "I should shut up. You probably think I'm being stupid."

"Not at all," he said honestly. "You're right. Things have never been weirder. Twilight Zone, for sure."

Jessie smiled. He had made her feel better. Not about the things that had taken place. But, Tyler made her feel like it was okay to be herself – no matter what that meant. It was a safe feeling. He had always made her feel that way, which is why she knew she shouldn't be surprised he had done so once again. She briefly wished Graham possessed that quality and then felt guilty for thinking such a thing, especially while he was laid up in the hospital. She just couldn't help it. Jessie found herself wanting to reach out and give Tyler a hug. But, she knew she shouldn't. What she didn't know was, if she had, Tyler would have been so delighted he might never have let her go.

Unaware of what Jessie was thinking and feeling at that moment, Tyler wanted to keep her from focusing on the strange events too much so he tried to change the subject. "You heading to lunch?"

"Actually," Jessie started, "I'm going to go over to the hospital to see Graham."

"He's in the hospital?"

"Yeah, you haven't heard that? I guess Coach Clark's coffee burned him pretty bad. They might even have to do a little surgery. Skin grafts or something."

"Are you serious?"

"Yeah."

Guilt quickly took hold of Tyler as he realized why some of the students had been expressing compassion for Graham rather than laughing about the incident. Word had begun to spread about how severely he had been burned. They were right to feel compassion. Tyler now knew that he was the one who was wrong. What he had done to Graham was no more justified than what Graham had done to him.

Adding to his guilt, the sight of Jessie feeling distraught hurt Tyler deeply and he became awkwardly quiet. Her sadness, however, was just one of the two major reasons that he was feeling ashamed. Perhaps even more significant was the fact that, where he felt justified before, his conscience was now beginning to make him feel like the bad guy in all of this. Tyler may not have started it but he had certainly taken steps to make sure that it was he who delivered the final blow. He knew he didn't have the right to decide who deserved punishment and how that punishment should be delivered. The god-like actions he'd taken felt good at the time but now he just felt ugly inside.

"Tell him I'm sorry about what happened," Tyler finally said.

"That's pretty nice of you, considering-"

"No," Tyler interrupted. "It's really not. Believe me. He deserved a comeuppance but he didn't deserve what happened to him this morning. That wasn't right. I'll see you later."

"Okay," Jessie said as she watched him leave in a hurry. She felt surprised and confused by Tyler's reaction. There was a connection between Tyler's accident and Graham's pep assembly fiasco that she knew she was missing. But, her mind quickly shifted from paranormal investigative reporter mode right back to the far more basic sympathy mode over Graham and his unfortunate plight.

Tyler kept walking without looking back at Jessie or, without really looking anywhere at anybody for that matter. He stared at the floor, feeling the weight of all that was happening. The light feeling of relief he had experienced only moments ago, had now been replaced with a very heavy feeling of regret. *Maybe I am the devil*, he contemplated.

CHAPTER TWENTY-SEVEN
Amazing

Heading outside for lunch, Tyler was simultaneously fighting bouts with regret, depression, sorrow, and self-criticism. In one short moment, he had gone from feeling justified in what he had done to Graham, to feeling absolutely terrible about it. Few people would argue with the fact that Graham was a complete jerk, but Tyler now knew beyond a shadow of a doubt that there was no excuse for what he had done to that cocky schmuck.

Tyler had not only humiliated Graham but he had also caused permanent physical damage. To hear that Graham may now need skin grafting to repair the damage he had caused was absolutely devastating to Tyler. He was now in a zombie state that closely resembled how Jessie looked just minutes earlier. But, where she was confused and sad, Tyler was overwhelmed with guilt. He didn't know if he was going to get feverishly sweaty or just upchuck right there in the hallway. The level of grief he was suffering as a result of his shame was beyond anything he had ever experienced before. It was as though he had lost a part of himself. He feared that his innocence and belief that he was a good person, were retreating from the safety and comfort of their home in his heart, similar to children choosing to become members of the gutter punk scene. Lost and scared of what he had become, Tyler didn't believe he would ever be able to forgive himself.

He knew that some people, Preston included, might find the idea of gaining these new abilities to be a cool and exciting thing to have happen to them. And, Tyler would admit that from a distance, it truly did sound like a really cool thing. But, up close and personal was something altogether different. He wanted nothing more at this moment than to go back to the way things were before this started happening to him. He couldn't possibly have known that he was just moments away from that desire escalating totally off the scale.

Tyler was so preoccupied with his self-deprecating thoughts that, at first, he didn't notice the obvious smell of stale french fries and grease-dripping pizza slices as he opened the cold metal door to go outside. As soon as he stepped through the doorway, he spotted Preston standing in front of a crowd of students who were placing money into his Seattle SuperSonics ball cap. Tyler immediately stopped as Preston spotted him.

"Here he comes," Preston barked in his best announcer voice, "ladies and gentlemen, the amazing Tyler!"

Tyler was frozen in fear and shock as the crowd spun around, waiting for him to put on a show. The only consolation for what he had done to Graham was the fact that people were no longer talking about him. Preston had clearly ruined that and put all eyes back on him. Rage welled up within Tyler like an erupting volcano but Tyler knew he had to contain it.

"He can move things with his mind," Preston continued, "read people's thoughts, see through walls and, he's even defeated death!"

Tyler broke through the crowd and charged forward until he was less than three inches from Preston's face. "What do you think you're doing?" he whispered, furiously.

"Trying to reel in a few dead presidents," Preston declared. "Don't worry, I'll split it with you. Show 'em the rock trick."

"It's not a trick," Tyler snapped. "There are no tricks. I can't even do most of the things you just said I can do."

"Don't be such a buzz crusher," Preston told Tyler as the crowd whispered to each other impatiently. "Just go with it. It's part of the act."

"What act?" Tyler asked, angrily. "This is my life you're selling. Have you forgotten our conversation?"

"Have you?" Preston fired back. "I told you to find a way to enjoy it. This is the way."

"No, it's not."

"Tyler…"

Tyler turned around to address the crowd. "If I could read people's thoughts, wouldn't I, at the very least, have a girlfriend? Think about it. For the first time in my life, I'd always know exactly what to say to a girl." Tyler paused briefly before continuing as the crowd finished chuckling at his joke. "Preston's full of crap, people. That can't come as a surprise to anyone. I'm not sure how he thought this was going to end but, you might want to get a refund."

"I knew it," a student expressed as the crowd stepped forward to pull their money back out of the hat.

Tyler turned around and leaned back into Preston's face with so much anger he looked like smoke might billow from his ears and fire might shoot out of his eyes. "If you ever come within ten feet of me or so much as speak my name to anyone again," he whispered indignantly, "I will make you wish you'd never met me. And believe me, that I can do."

"I was just…" Preston trailed off as Tyler walked away, leaving Preston unable to defend himself. "I was trying to help," Preston sincerely told himself. He was completely mortified by what he had just done to his best friend. Of course, he thought he could benefit from his scheme. But, he honestly saw it going totally differently. He really did want to help Tyler embrace and ultimately enjoy this new chapter in his life. Clearly, he had failed in all regards. Between the two of them, it seemed as if Preston and Tyler were hoarding all of the guilt in Penuel.

Tyler turned a corner and almost ran Mr. Russell over. "Oh," Tyler reacted. "Sorry, Mr. Russell."

"Hey, that's okay. No, problem." Mr. Russell responded. As Tyler started to walk away, Mr. Russell stopped him with his words. "Actually, I'd like to talk to you if you have a minute."

"Sure," Tyler said both reluctantly and skeptically.

"Tyler, you've barely been making C's in my class all year long."

"I know," Tyler admitted, embarrassed.

"I just corrected the test you took this morning."

"Yeah?" Tyler asked with increased skepticism.

"You got a perfect score," Mr. Russell told him in disbelief.

"No way," Tyler reacted, showing authentic delight on his face.

"Can you explain that?"

"Well," Tyler hesitated, "I, uh. Well, I, since the accident, I haven't been able to sleep much. I've just been using my extra time to read a lot more. I guess it paid off."

"So, you wouldn't mind re-taking it?" Mr. Russell proposed.

"Not at all," Tyler said emphatically, suddenly feeling

confident. "Let's do it right now."

"Not necessary," Mr. Russell told Tyler, having heard exactly what he wanted to hear but still feeling a hint of uncertainty. "I just hope you're telling me the truth, Tyler. You're a good kid. I'd hate to have to bust you on this."

"You won't," Tyler tried to reassure him. "I promise, Mr. Russell."

"Good," Mr. Russell said as he started to walk away. "Then keep up the good work. I'll expect the same results on the next test."

"You've got it," Tyler said. "Thanks." Tyler turned and walked away. *At least something went right today,* he thought.

The feeling of joy over the success on his test was quickly replaced by the far stronger feeling that the rest of his life was falling apart. He'd done something devious in hurting Graham to the point of hospitalization and now he'd lost his jerk of a best friend. *What's next?* he wondered.

CHAPTER TWENTY-EIGHT
Free Will

If it weren't for his mom, Tyler would feel just as alone emotionally as he was physically while walking home from school that afternoon. The only other person who knew what was happening to him had now betrayed him. And, to make matters far worse, he felt he had betrayed himself by causing permanent damage to Graham. No matter how big of a jerk Graham was, and he was probably the biggest living jerk Tyler knew about, Tyler should have known better than to do what he did to him. He had let his emotions, frustrations and anger get the best of him. This was rare for Tyler. He wasn't normally prone to emotional outbursts. But, this thing with Graham had been building inside of Tyler for years and the volcano had finally erupted. And now, in the aftermath, Tyler was having a very hard time forgiving himself for it.

He turned a corner, mind racing, and strolled up the street toward his house. As he approached the driveway, he saw an elderly woman climb out of the passenger side of a blue 1988 Ford Escort Station Wagon and his heart nearly leapt out of his chest.

As she climbed out, her face was turned down and away. Her head also disappeared behind the door for a moment and the glaring sun helped to keep her identity hidden at first. So, he initially thought it might be the woman his mom told him about having seen twenty-five years ago and then again in the grocery store the night before. But, as he regained his composure and the woman came into view, he recognized her as Nancy Hanley.

"Mrs. Hanley…" Tyler said out loud.

"Hello, Tyler," she responded joyfully.

"What's going on?" Tyler asked, growing concerned. "Is everything okay? Are you alright?"

"I've never been better, Tyler."

"Good," Tyler said, as concern turned first into relief and then into good old-fashioned curiosity. He glanced back at the station wagon she arrived in and noticed a woman about the same age waiting for her in the driver's seat. "Can I help you with something?"

"I just had to come by and say thank you."

"But, you already have, Mrs. Hanley. Quite a few times."

"Not just for saving my physical life. You've done so much more than that, Tyler. You have also saved my spiritual life. What you did for me restored my faith in God."

"Mrs. Hanley…" Tyler tried to butt in but Nancy kept going, intent on saying what she came to say.

"God and I haven't talked much since my husband Richard died. I really didn't have much to say to the Almighty after that. I just didn't understand. Still don't. But, I'm okay with that now. I think that's why God put me in that car on that highway at that moment. So I could meet you. It was the Lord's way of saying He wanted to get our conversation going again. And, it worked. I'm so thankful, Tyler. Talking with God again has filled me with the love I was missing after Richard died."

"Mrs. Hanley," Tyler started again, trying to stop her from giving him far more credit than he felt he deserved. "I don't…"

"Tyler," she interrupted, "I don't know what you are."

The statement surprised him. He was trying to figure that one out about himself, too.

"Maybe you're an angel," she continued. "Maybe you're just a boy that God chose to use for a miracle. I really don't know."

Me neither, he thought with the weight of guilt still resting squarely on the shoulders of his conscience. *I also might be something quite the opposite.*

"What I do know," Mrs. Hanley continued, "is that I owe

you my life. To a certain extent, I owe you my soul. And, all I know how to do in return is say thank you, thank you, thank you."

Mrs. Hanley leaned forward and hugged Tyler. She kissed him on the cheek and then climbed into the station wagon without another word. Her friend started the engine back up and they drove away with just the exchange of a wave as they went.

Tyler stood in the driveway for a moment, awestruck by the timing of Nancy's visit. Instead of going inside like he intended, he sat down in the front yard and stared up at the heavens. *Why is this happening to me?* he wondered as he kicked off his shoes and socks. Tyler wondered if Nancy was right. Was it possible that, somehow, God could have something to do with this whole crazy thing? Or, maybe Nancy *was* the crazy thing.

He shoved his feet in the dirt, sifting it with his toes. It felt like such a natural thing to do that it didn't even dawn on him that this was something he had really never done before. It simultaneously calmed him down and gave him a boost of energy.

Without warning, he stood up and started running in his bare feet. He ran fast, hard, and for an impossibly long distance. Tyler ran through the entire town, passing through industrial parks, residential areas, commercial and business parks. He ran over highways and through Main Street. He ran along the highway where the accident had taken place and then sprinted away from it as if that would somehow take him away from all that had happened. The only time Tyler stopped running was briefly at a bank on the Yakima River where he stared at the water for a moment before looking up to the heavens once again. That's when he finally screamed at God, "What do you want from me?!" He wasn't about to wait for a response he didn't expect to come. In fact, it probably would have caused him to wet his pants if an audible response had been given.

The rain began to pour down as Tyler started to run again. Afternoon had turned into evening and evening was now becoming night as darkness snuffed out the daylight.

Tyler had reached his emotional limit. He couldn't figure out if he was good or evil. He didn't know if he had been given a gift by God, been possessed by a demon, or if he was just some freak accident that had nothing to do with anything. *What do I do?* he asked himself as he ran into a park and finally came to a stop for only the second time since he had left his yard.

He found himself sitting underneath an old evergreen tree, semi-shielded from the rain. His head was draped forward over his legs from emotional exhaustion. He could no longer tell his tears from the rain that soaked his skin. He sat back and leaned against the tree trunk, breathing deeply. He stared up at the rain falling from the dark sky with so many more questions than answers and both the words of Nancy Hanley and the story of his mom's supposed prophetess fighting his inner demons for attention.

Wiping the rain and tears from his eyes, Tyler leaned his head forward and looked straight ahead for the first time since sitting down under the tree. He noticed that the Kittitas Valley Healthcare Hospital was about five hundred feet directly in front of him.

Tyler stood up again as he realized he had run all the way to Ellensburg. *That must be about fifty miles,* he pondered. *Maybe I'm Forrest Gump.* The smile muscles in his cheek put up a fight at the thought but, ultimately, his emotions won the battle and Tyler stared blankly at the hospital. Leaving the umbrella protection of the tree and getting drenched again, he headed toward the hospital.

Tyler didn't care about the rain. He was too focused on the sense of peace that was finally coming over him. He realized that whatever the reason for his newfound abilities, he had the capacity to choose what to do with them. Therefore, who he would be from this moment forward was up to him. And, what he decided to do with those abilities would determine exactly who that was.

CHAPTER TWENTY-NINE
Undone

Dripping water from every inch of his body, Tyler stepped into the hospital and looked around. Clearly, visiting hours were over. But, something was off. The place was eerily quiet.

Finally, he spotted two nurses, who he assumed would normally be sitting at the front desk. Instead, they were standing in front of the waiting room TV along with a man who Tyler assumed was the family member of a patient. They were all glued to a breaking news story.

"No one knows the cause of the fire as of yet," came the news reporter's voice from the TV. "What we do know is that it started somewhere in the Central Chilean Andes no more than eight hours ago."

The nurses were so entranced by the story that they didn't even see Tyler walk right behind them and continue quietly down the hallway. He kept his chin in his chest and his face away from the security cameras, leaving a trail of water with every step. Tyler leapt into a corner and hid behind the doorframe as a mammoth-sized security guard turned down the hallway just a few feet away from him.

The security guard disappeared from view and Tyler poked his head out. He saw a camera hanging from the ceiling on the other side of the doorframe, reached his hand out and, with a little concentration, shattered the lens. He telekinetically swept the glass into the corner opposite him and stepped into the adjoining hallway, where the security guard had come from.

Peeking into the windows as he walked, Tyler snuck down the hallway until he found the room he wanted. He opened the door and stepped quietly inside.

Graham was lying asleep as Tyler closed the door behind him before walking over to the bed. He glanced around nervously as Graham's eyes slowly began to open.

"What the… What are you doing here?" Graham asked, suspiciously.

"Fixing something I shouldn't have done," Tyler answered him, honestly.

"What's that?" Graham asked as he struggled to sit up. "And why are you so wet? You look like you swam here."

"Just lay down," Tyler insisted as he put his right hand on Graham's chest and pushed him back down against the mattress.

"Don't touch me, queer!" Graham shouted as he tried to sit back up. "What are you gonna do? Get your hand off of me!"

"I'm not afraid of you anymore," Tyler said, continuing to calmly hold him down. "I've realized something, Graham. You're afraid of me."

"What?"

"And you know what?"

"What, Greg Louganis?"

"You should be very afraid of me."

"Why would I be afraid of-"

"Just lay there," Tyler said, cutting Graham off. "I'm here to help you."

"Help me? Yeah, right. How could you possibly help me?"

Tyler reached his left arm out and laid his hand on Graham's crotch.

"I knew it!" Graham yelled. "Get your hands off of me, fag!"

Graham's eyes began to bug out as both he and Tyler felt the energy being exchanged. It was so intense it nearly lifted Graham up off of the bed. After a moment, Graham's body relaxed. He caught his breath and realized that the pain he had been feeling was now completely gone.

"What did you just do to me?" Graham asked, staring at Tyler. He then looked down and lifted the bed sheet to check himself. "The burns are gone," Graham said in amazement before looking back up at Tyler. "What did you do to me, freak?"

"I fixed it."

"What are you, some kind of friggin' alien or somethin'?"

"I don't know what I am. And, you don't need to know. If you ever tell anybody what just happened, I'll put it back. Only next time I'll make it worse. You understand?"

Graham became quiet and nearly motionless. He simply nodded in agreement as Tyler backed away and left the room. He stepped back into the hallway, checking to make sure the coast was clear, and closed the door behind him.

Sneaking down the hallway, Tyler blew out another camera lens just before he came into view. He swept the glass into a corner as he walked past it undetected.

Tyler noticed a sign that read: Intensive Care Unit. He paused for a moment and sighed, feeling a weight of responsibility. With a heavy head, he made the decision to change course, and he was quickly off and moving cautiously in the direction the sign had pointed.

Poking his head around the corner, Tyler saw a small group of doctors and nurses gathered around a TV watching the same breaking news story the two nurses at the hospital's entrance were watching.

"The fire grew at a rate of over a hundred square kilometers or twenty-five thousand acres per hour," came the same news reporter's voice from the TV, "completely mystifying experts, and by now should have consumed much if not all of Santiago."

Tyler was paying little attention to the news story as he felt drawn to the patients in the various rooms. He somehow felt needed by them. He opened the first door and snuck inside, closing the door behind him.

Approaching the patient who occupied the room, a sleeping hairless twelve year-old boy, Tyler picked up the clipboard attached at the end of the bed. He read that the boy had been diagnosed with acute leukemia at the age of six. The next thing to jump out at him was the word *terminal.* As he set the clipboard down, his eyes filled with tears. He couldn't help but think about the fact that this child had, so far, missed out on a normal childhood. The doctors had apparently determined that this wouldn't change.

Tyler knew differently.

He reached both hands out and began to heal him the same way he healed Graham and Nancy. As it had been with both Graham and Nancy, the energy exchange was significant. This time, the boy actually lifted about an inch off of the bed. When he was finished, the boy settled gently back into the bed, woke up, and simply smiled at Tyler, warmly and appreciatively.

Tyler visited every room in the I.C.U. that night. He healed every patient, all with different but severe afflictions. With each patient healed, Tyler grew weaker. It was an exhausting process, but what it took away in energy, it gave back to Tyler in purpose. This is exactly what Tyler had been missing. Before he entered the hospital, Tyler couldn't understand why this was all happening to him. Simply noticing the sign that pointed the way to the I.C.U. had changed that. And, with it, everything else. Tyler's world would never be the same again.

Finally, he stumbled out of the last room and tried to make it out of the I.C.U. undetected.

"Less than half an hour ago," the news reporter's voice continued from the TV, "the whole thing simply vanished into thin air. The fire seems to have totally evaporated and no one knows how or why. Although, some locals claim to have seen what they are calling a vision of the Mother Mary…"

Tyler only made it as far as the group of doctors and nurses who were still watching the T.V. before he collapsed to the floor. He was sweating and panting from fatigue, causing everyone to spin around and rush to his aid as he ultimately passed out in front of them.

CHAPTER THIRTY
Exposed

As Tyler gently regained consciousness, he heard voices talking quietly. His eyes slowly opened and he realized that he was still in the hospital. In fact, he was now in his own room, lying in a hospital bed and hooked up to an I.V. He looked to his left, as his eyes progressively focused, to see who was talking. He gradually spotted a doctor, a nurse and Sheriff Wilson standing just a few feet away.

"He appears to be suffering from an extreme case of fatigue," the doctor told the sheriff.

"Well," the sheriff responded, "as you know, this boy's been through a lot this week and his mother tells me he hasn't really slept since the accident. If I were him, I'd be exhausted, too."

"I understand and I'm inclined to agree. Anxiety is a common cause of fatigue and he has every reason to be experiencing anxiety after that accident. I'm still trying to wrap my head around that one, by the way. However, I haven't gotten to the really strange part about tonight yet, Sheriff…" the doctor began to say but glanced at Tyler and noticed that he was awake. "Hey, feeling any better?"

"I feel cashed," Tyler said before clearing his throat and using all of his facial muscles to try and widen his eyes.

The doctor looked at the sheriff, confused by Tyler's use of the slang term *cashed*.

"I think that means burned out so, that's a no," the sheriff told the doctor. "Doc, could I have a moment alone with Tyler?"

"Sure, I'll be in the hallway when you're done," the doctor answered the sheriff before turning his attention back to Tyler. "I'll be back to see you in a few minutes and we'll run some tests. See if we can't uncash you." The doctor awkwardly looked around to see if anyone was proud of him for the use of the slang term. When he got no response, he realized he had likely used it incorrectly and turned to leave without another word.

"Thanks," the sheriff told the doctor before grabbing a chair and scooting it closer to Tyler. He sat down and started speaking to Tyler in a friendly but serious tone. "We've got a lot to talk about, you and me."

"Yeah, sorry I haven't made it into the station yet."

"Forget about that. Let's start with what you're doing here tonight."

"I came to see Graham," Tyler answered, honestly.

"The quarterback with the coffee burns? I didn't know you two were friends."

"We're not. Not even close."

"So, why would you come to see him?"

"Guess I felt sorry for him."

"Can't fault you for being nice. Did you know visiting hours were over?"

"No," Tyler lied. "Have I committed a crime?"

"I'm not arresting you, Tyler. I'm just asking you a few questions."

"That's a relief. I thought maybe I'd violated a city ordinance against kindness."

"Well, I'm Sheriff of Penuel. County's out of my jurisdiction. I suppose I could arrest you for being a sarcastic little punk but, for now, I think I'll just chalk that up to you being tired. Sound fair?"

"Very," Tyler said sheepishly. Sheriff Wilson had never taken that tone with him before and the jolt of it let Tyler know he was out of line. "Sorry."

"All good," the sheriff said, ready to move on. Continuing to press… "So, your visit with Graham didn't have anything to do with the accident?"

"Well, I saw it happen. But, so did the rest of the school. It was kind of funny at first, until I heard how serious his burns were. But, he says he's doing better now so, I guess that's good."

"That's fine and all, Tyler. But, I'm referring to *your* accident."

"Why would it have anything to do with my accident?" Tyler inquired.

"Well, for starters, because I know he was there."

Tyler swallowed, nervously, then asked, "What makes you say that?"

"I traced some fresh tire marks on the highway to three cars in Douglas County. I took the pictures and showed them to Nancy Hanley. She identified Graham's as having been there. Plus, your car was covered in eggs. I'm assuming neither you, nor Nancy, did that."

Tyler was silent.

"I know Graham caused the accident," the sheriff told Tyler. "I'm just waiting for you to say it."

"I don't want to press any charges," Tyler finally said, unequivocally.

The sheriff was appalled but tried his best to hide it. "Why not?"

"He's paid for it."

"Not according to the law," the sheriff stated, ardently.

"Isn't it my decision?"

"And Nancy Hanley's."

"She can press charges if she wants to. I don't. But, I won't try and talk her out of it either. I wouldn't blame her if she did."

"Good," the sheriff said sincerely while still deep in thought. Finally, after a moment of silence, he let Tyler in on what he was contemplating. "I guess I just don't understand how Graham has paid for causing the accident. How is what happened to him, in any way related to what happened to you?"

"It isn't," Tyler lied again.

"See what I mean. I just don't get it."

"It doesn't matter. You don't need to understand."

"Okay," the sheriff conceded. "So, tell me how you wound up in the I.C.U."

After a deep breath, Tyler began to explain. "I was on my way back out of the hospital."

"So, you had already seen Graham?"

"Yes. That's when he told me he was feeling better."

Ignoring another snarky comment, the sheriff continued to push. "How did you get in after visiting hours in the first place?"

"No one was at the reception desk. I think everyone was distracted by the news. Some fire in Chile or something."

"Yeah, that is a major ordeal right now. Some might say it's even more miraculous than your car accident." The sheriff was testing the waters. He waited for a response but didn't get one so he decided to keep the conversation moving. "Okay, so you went and saw Graham. Then what?"

"I left and I got dizzy in the hallway. I must've stumbled in there and passed out. I really don't remember very much. I was pretty out of it."

"That's quite a stumble," the sheriff said as he stood up, suspicious of Tyler's story. "I'll tell you what, you keep resting and I'll be back in a minute to talk to you some more. I just need to find out a little more from the good doctor out there, okay?"

"Sure," Tyler agreed.

"Alright," the sheriff said as he started to walk out. "I guess I'd better give your mom a call, too."

"Sheriff?"

"Yeah?"

"Could you wait on that?"

"Why?"

"Just for a little while. I don't want her to worry."

"She's long since been home from work by now, Tyler. She has to be wondering where you are. With everything she already knows has gone on with you lately, she must be worried. I can't put it off much longer. Unless, of course, you want to do it."

"Yeah, I'll do it. Just give me a few more minutes to wake up and collect my thoughts."

"Fine. I'll be right back. We still have some things to cover.

I want to hear about your conversation with Graham and I'm quite curious as to how you got from Penuel all the way out here to the hospital in the first place. School had only been out for about four hours when you collapsed so, I'm pretty confident you didn't walk all the way out here. Back in five."

The sheriff walked out and Tyler immediately pulled the I.V. out of his left arm. He climbed out of bed and quickly realized that his arm was bleeding where he had ripped the I.V. out. He rushed to the counter and grabbed some gauze, soaked some blood up and tossed it in the garbage. He placed some more gauze on his arm and pressed firmly. He reached up to the cupboards on the wall with his left arm and opened two before finding what he wanted. He pulled some medical tape out and wrapped it around his arm a couple of times to hold the gauze in place. He tore the tape and walked over to the closet. He grabbed his clothes and tossed them on the bed. Tyler clearly had no intention of being there when Sherriff Wilson returned.

CHAPTER THIRTY-ONE
Escape

The door to Tyler's hospital room opened slightly and Tyler slowly inched his head through the crack. Now dressed in his still mostly damp street clothes, Tyler looked to his right and spotted the door that he knew he needed to get through. He then looked to his left and saw the sheriff and the doctor, with their backs to him, talking to one another about twenty feet down the hall. They were speaking softly in an attempt to make sure no one else could hear them. But, Tyler focused on their voices and, like the girls in the high school parking lot, the conversation sounded as though they were right next to him.

"Every single patient in the I.C.U. is suddenly in perfect health," the doctor told the sheriff in complete amazement. Tyler allowed the corners of his mouth to turn up just slightly. He couldn't help but feel good knowing he had been successful in doing the right thing. There would be no regretting his decision to help those people. He had no doubt that this action was a far better path than the one he had started down by attacking Graham at the pep assembly. But, now he had to find a way to escape the inevitable consequences of people finding out about him. The doctor continued, "The tests we're running are so far coming up empty. We can't find anything wrong with any of them. We're talking terminal patients suddenly as healthy as you and I. I've never seen… I've never even heard of anything like it in my life."

"Are you saying you think Tyler had something to do with that?" asked the sheriff.

As their conversation continued, Tyler knew he had a limited opportunity while their attention was on each other. He snuck quickly through the door and hurried stealthily down the hallway without being detected.

Completely unaware of Tyler's departure, the doctor thoughtfully answered the sheriff's inquiry. "I'm saying that miracles seem to follow that boy wherever he goes lately. Now, we've done every test we can think of and they haven't revealed anything out of the ordinary about Tyler's DNA or anything else."

"Of course not, Doc. Why would you think they would?"

"Normally, I wouldn't. As a man of science I…" The doctor stopped himself and thought long and hard about what he was saying to the sheriff. He concluded that he had no explanation and knew that admitting it was the only thing he could do at this point. "A couple of hours ago I thought they would find some logical explanation for what happened in both Japan and Chile. That boy in there, all by himself, has me questioning… What if we have our own miracle happening right here in Kittitas County? If you knew me, Sheriff, you'd know just how profound a question like that coming from me truly is. Tyler Hirsch has me questioning absolutely everything I thought I knew. And, for maybe the first time in my entire adult life, I have no idea what to do or even what to believe right now."

Tyler heard every word of their conversation up to that point but he stopped listening as he rounded a corner near the hospital entrance and shifted his focus to his exit. He tried to act as normal as a young man experiencing what he was going through possibly could. He swiftly changed his stealth hustle into a casual walk as he headed toward the electric doors that led to his supposed freedom. Unfortunately, it wasn't enough.

One of the two nurses who had been watching the breaking news story when Tyler first arrived had moved behind the front desk. She spied Tyler and briefly wondered who this stranger was exiting the building so long after visiting hours. Suddenly, she remembered hearing about the teenager who collapsed outside of I.C.U. and then recalled that he was the one who the sheriff had come to see. She hastily decided she needed to try and stop him. "Excuse me," the nurse called out. "Sir, are you a patient here?"

At first, Tyler completely ignored her and just kept moving toward the door. He tried to pretend he didn't hear anything but couldn't help increasing his pace which, of course, only made him look more suspicious.

"Sir?" she tried again as she grabbed her hand radio and came out from behind the desk. "I don't think I have any release forms for you."

"You don't," Tyler finally answered as he approached the doors.

The nurse started walking toward Tyler as she put her walkie-talkie to her mouth and clicked the button to speak. "Bernie? That teenager from I.C.U.'s trying to rabbit. Smoke break's over."

As Tyler stepped outside, the same mammoth-sized security guard he'd seen in a hallway earlier put his cigarette out and stepped in front of Tyler.

"Sir," Bernie said in a booming voice, "I've been instructed not to let you leave."

"Instructed by who?" Tyler asked. "I'm not a prisoner. Please step aside. I can't stay here."

"Fine. Just let me clear it with Sheriff Wilson."

"With all due respect," Tyler interrupted, "you're a security guard, not a cop. And, in Ellensburg, Sheriff Wilson is out of his jurisdiction."

As the nurse approached the two of them, Bernie leaned in to Tyler, getting less than three inches from his face like he was about to start a fight. "That didn't sound very respectful to me."

"Sorry," Tyler asserted, "But, you don't want to do that. Woah. Especially not with smoker's breath. Smells like there might be a little salami in there, too."

The nurse failed as she tried to hold back the laughter, embarrassing Bernie and making him angry. "Feels about right to me," Bernie said, defiantly. "What are you gonna do about it, funny boy?"

"Clever," Tyler said as he reached forward. Bernie tried to swat Tyler's hand away but was unable to make him budge. He tried again. No response. Despite Bernie's severe protest, Tyler managed to grab hold of his shirt with one hand and lift him a foot and a half off the ground.

"Oh," the nurse let out in total shock.

Tyler rotated Bernie from in front of him to behind him, directly beside the nurse, and then set him back down.

"I told you," Tyler maintained, "I can't stay here."

"Okay," Bernie conceded, stunned by Tyler's brute strength.

As Tyler took off running and ultimately disappeared into the shadows, the sheriff ran around the corner in the hallway, through the lobby, and out of the electric doors, furious as he realized he was too late and Tyler was gone.

"Dog-gone it, Bernie!" the sheriff shouted. "Kid's not even half your size."

"He's the strongest person I've ever seen, though," Bernie told the sheriff. "Lifted me clean off the ground with one hand."

"Uh-huh," the nurse agreed, still stunned by the whole event.

It took a moment to register with the sheriff, but it finally surfaced in his brain as he looked Bernie's massive body up and down. "Wait, what did you just say?"

"I swear it's true, Sheriff."

"It is," the nurse agreed again.

"I believe you," the sheriff admitted. He turned and looked back out into the darkness. "God help me, I actually believe you."

CHAPTER THIRTY-TWO
Committing

The sheriff went straight to Kathleen's house and knocked on the front door. He felt terrible when she answered looking extremely anxious. Kathleen had been home from work and unable to locate Tyler for several hours now and the sight of the sheriff and the fact that he didn't have Tyler with him only increased her level of panic. She was just barely holding her emotions at bay and was on the verge of coming undone.

"Oh Ron," she let out, "I tried to call you but you weren't at the station. Is he okay?"

"I don't know where he is, Kathleen," the sheriff admitted as he made a mental note of the need to get city approval to add cell phones to the police budget. Letting that go to focus on the present, he motioned inside and asked, "May I?"

"Of course. I'm sorry." Kathleen stepped aside to let the sheriff in and closed the door behind him. "I called Preston and he said they had a fight at school today. He hasn't heard from him since. He's always here when I come home from work."

"I've seen him more recently than you have."

"What do you mean?"

"That's why I'm here."

"What is it? What's wrong? Is he okay?"

"Kathleen, there are some things going on around Tyler that I just don't understand."

"You mean the accident?"

"And tonight."

"What happened tonight, Ron? I'm freaking out here."

"It's okay. When I saw him, he was fine."

"Then tell me what happened."

"Tyler snuck into the hospital and collapsed in the I.C.U."

"Oh, my…"

"He woke up fine. Doctors said he simply collapsed from exhaustion. Or, fatigue I think they called it. Whatever. Same thing. Anyway, they called me in because of the car accident."

"You know he hasn't been sleeping."

"That's what I told them."

"Why didn't the hospital call me?"

"I told them I would."

"But, you didn't."

"Tyler told me he would."

"But, he didn't either. I'm his mother and he's a minor. I'm the last person who should be left in the dark.”

“You’re absolutely right. And, when he fled the hospital, I drove straight here.”

“Why would he flee the hospital?”

“That ties itself into one of my big questions in all of this.”

“Which is?” Kathleen asked, somewhat hesitantly.

“Tyler said he was there visiting a boy from the high school that had been burned pretty badly this morning by some spilled coffee. Everyone in that I.C.U., including terminal patients and that burn victim from the high school, all miraculously healed from their afflictions tonight. You add that to the car accident and tell me what I’m supposed to be thinking right now.”

Kathleen looked like a kid caught with her hand in the cookie jar. She knew the sheriff to be a smart man. He may not know exactly what was going on with Tyler, at least not any more than she or Tyler did, but he had correctly put together the pieces of the puzzle that he did have. She could also tell that he knew she was aware of things she wasn’t sharing with him. “Where is that kid?” she wondered out loud, mostly because she really wanted to know the answer but she was clearly also using the question as a deflection.

“I hope you know,” the sheriff started, “I would never do anything to bring harm to you or your boy.”

“I do,” Kathleen said. She meant it, too. The sheriff was a

good man and she knew deep down that she could trust him. But, it was still difficult. The stakes couldn't be any higher. This, after all, was her precious son Tyler's life.

It was quiet for a moment while they were both deep in thought until the sheriff decided to pry in another direction.

"You mind if I ask you something personal?" he asked her. "It might be a touchy subject so, you don't have to answer if you don't want to."

"Go ahead."

"I didn't know Brett Riggle all that well. Obviously, being that he's Tyler's father, you did. For a time, anyway."

Kathleen was taken aback. She couldn't have seen this coming. "Uh, yeah. Yeah, I certainly did."

"He left town before Tyler was born, right?" The sheriff asked this question even though he already knew the answer.

"That's right," Kathleen responded, knowing that she wasn't giving the sheriff any information he didn't already have and wondering where he was going with this line of questions.

"Has he been in touch at all since?"

"Not so much as a birthday card."

"Sorry," the sheriff acknowledged. Feeling a bit guilty for opening the wound, he decided he'd better add some condolences along with his statement of disapproval. "That ain't right."

"He's a first rate jerk. No question about it. But, I actually think he made things easier for us that way. Trust me, that wasn't his intention. He was always all about himself. But, him leaving and staying away turned out to be the best thing that ever happened to both Tyler and I."

The sheriff was only slightly surprised and a little bit pleased by her response. What little he knew of Brett, he didn't like. But, that wasn't his end game here. He was still trying to get to the heart of what was happening with Tyler. "You don't suppose that, whatever's going on with Tyler is inherited, do you?"

"I can say for certain it didn't come from me and I'm equally confident there was never anything special about Brett."

"Fair enough." Another moment of silence passed while more deep thoughts ran through their minds. Each was well aware of the fact that she had begun to let the sheriff in by admitting that there was, indeed, something going on with Tyler. Kathleen wasn't sure she should let him in any further and the sheriff knew that he flat out needed more in order to be able to protect Tyler properly. Finally, he spoke again, needing to get something off of his chest. "You and Tyler don't have to go through this alone. You know that, right? I'm here to help… If you'll let me. But, I need to know whatever it is you're holding back in order to do that."

"I'm trying to protect my son, Ron."

"So am I."

"Okay," Kathleen finally agreed. She paused a minute while each of them mentally braced themselves for the confession that was coming. Finally, she started in. "Your suspicions about the accident are down the line accurate. But, let me be clear that there has never been any sign of anything like this until this week. I can't tell you about what happened in the hospital tonight because I didn't know anything about it. But, I'd be willing to bet Tyler healed those people, too. He's a gift, Ron. Not just to me. To all of us. That has recently become abundantly clear to me."

"I can see that, Kathleen. I get it. Tyler's going to need to be protected. There're a lot of people who're going to want a piece of him. We may even have to take him into hiding somewhere."

"We?"

"I told you. I'm here to help. I'm in. All the way."

"Thank you, Ron." Kathleen's emotions began to get the better of her. Tears welled up and she knew that she wouldn't be able to fight them much longer.

"I care about you, Kathleen. Always have. But, understand that this isn't just about that. I care about Tyler, too. I want to make sure he's safe."

"We don't know what's happening to him," Kathleen said as she lost the battle to hold back the tears and started to sob. "He's all alone out there.

CHAPTER THIRTY-THREE
The Third Reveal

Tyler ambled down a familiar street and, ultimately, found himself standing on the sidewalk in front of a house he had visited many times, but not for many years. He stared at it for several minutes, wondering what to do. Tyler was feeling better about the person he had decided to be. But, he still didn't know what his future held. He didn't know where to go or what to do. He certainly didn't know who to tell what was going on. The one thing he did know was that he wanted his future to involve Jessie.

He stepped off of the sidewalk and into a flowerbed where he curled his toes and let the dirt seep in and out of the spaces between them. The process gave him a level of comfort that he had only recently discovered in the midst of all of the chaos that now enveloped his life. He stared briefly at the window in Jessie's bedroom and noticed that the pink drapes she'd had when she was a kid had been replaced with white blinds. It was a reminder that so much had changed as they had grown up. If change could be viewed as a stovetop, the last few days felt as though someone had turned the dial to hi and the pot was suddenly boiling over.

After about a minute of gathering courage, he stepped out of the flowerbed and snuck up to the side of the house. He took a deep breath, scooped up a few pieces of mulch, and threw one at Jessie's window.

Jessie was sitting on top of the covers on her bed. She was doing homework when she heard the first piece of mulch hit her window. Having immediately looked toward the sound, she was staring at the window and feeling unsure of what she had heard when the second piece hit.

She slowly got up and nervously made her way to the window. She knew it couldn't be Graham because he was still in the hospital. She opened her window and poked her head out just as Tyler threw a third piece of mulch.

When he saw her, he telekinetically re-directed the mulch slightly so it hit the nearby window frame instead of her forehead.

Jessie glanced at the piece of mulch that narrowly missed her and then looked back down to see who it was throwing it. She was stunned when she recognized Tyler.

"Tyler?" she inquired in a stage whisper.

"Hey," he said at about the same volume.

"Hi," Jessie said, trying to lead Tyler to explain his presence.

"Were you asleep?"

"No," she answered, realizing he wasn't taking the bait. "I was studying. What are you doing here, besides throwing things at me?"

"I need to come inside."

"My dad would kill me if I let a boy in the house," she stated emphatically. "It's after midnight."

"Jessie, it's me."

Hesitating for a moment, she finally caved in. "Fine. I'll meet you around back."

Jessie disappeared back into her room, shutting the window behind her, as Tyler walked around to the back of the house and up to the sliding glass door. After a moment, Jessie appeared holding a cup of coffee and opened the door. "Come on in. Just keep it quiet."

"Thanks."

"You want a cup of coffee?" she asked as she led him to the couch.

"Do you have de-caf?"

"I don't think so."

"Better not," he said as they both sat down. "I've had enough trouble sleeping lately."

"Okay, tell me everything."

"I'm scared to."

"Tyler, you came here to tell me something."

"I came here because I didn't have anywhere else to go."

"Now that we've established you know how to make a girl feel special…"

"Jessie, we've barely spoken in like six or seven years."

"I know. That's my fault."

"It's nobody's fault."

"Yeah, it is. That's on me and I'm sorry."

"Forget about it."

"I can't."

"Would it help if I said you're forgiven?"

"Big time."

"You are," Tyler reassured her. They shared a brief smile and everything was silent for a moment while they both tried to figure out where to go from there. "I can't tell you what's going on with me right now," Tyler finally blurted out. "I can't really tell anyone."

"Then why are you here?" she asked, irritated by the obvious contradiction in his presence and secretiveness. "Why can't you go home? Why can't you go to Preston's?"

"Preston is a dangling hemorrhoid and they'll be looking for me at home."

"No argument about Preston, but who's they?"

No response.

"This doesn't have anything to do with Graham, does it?" Jessie asked.

"Not the way you'd think it does," Tyler finally spoke.

"Look, I want to help you. But, if you don't tell me what's going on, how can you expect me to do that?"

"Maybe you're right," Tyler said as he stood up and started to leave. "Maybe I shouldn't have come here."

"Does your mom know you're gone?"

"I left before she got home from work."

"She must be worried about you right now."

Tyler turned back around to face Jessie.

"If you don't have anywhere else to go…" Jessie started. "I never stopped caring about you, Tyler. In fact, I've really missed you." Embarrassed, Jessie's head dropped and she slowly reached for her cup of coffee.

Tyler knew he was being ridiculously indecisive but he couldn't imagine this would be easy for anyone. In that split second, he made his decision.

All of a sudden, the cup of coffee slid into Jessie's hand. She jumped back in shock. "Oh, my… Did you see that?"

"Yeah," Tyler answered casually. "I did."

Jessie looked at him with her mental wheels turning like they were on a Formula One racecar. "Why aren't you freaked out?"

"Because this is what's been going on with me."

"What is?"

"I shouldn't have survived that accident."

"What does that have to do with the coffee cup?"

"Everything. It's all… different. I'm different."

"You're Tyler. I've known you my whole life."

"None of this started happening to me until the morning of my accident."

"The same day as the football field incident?"

"Yeah."

"Show me again."

"Look down."

Jessie looked down and realized that the couch was hovering about a foot off of the ground.

"Okay, put me down, put me down."

They both giggled and Tyler shushed Jessie as the couch gently settled back onto the floor.

"This can't be real," Jessie said, enthusiastically. "Did I fall asleep? Am I dreaming this?"

"I wish you were."

"Why? This is fantastic."

"Not if people find out."

"They don't have to," Jessie told him.

"The doctors, some patients, and Sheriff Wilson already have."

"Just deny it. Can they prove anything?"

"I guess not," Tyler agreed.

"So, you're fine. You're better than fine. You're Superman and no one knows it but your mom and the original Musketeers. Although, if you're Superman, then that makes us more like The Justice League or something, huh?"

"I knew there was still some geek in there."

"You be quiet."

"Unfortunately, one of the Musketeers has a big mouth."

"Let me deal with the dangling hemorrhoid. But, I think you'd better give your mom a call. At least let her know you're okay."

"She'll like that I'm with you," he told her, causing a shared smile that began the mending of his heart.

CHAPTER THIRTY-FOUR
Circle Of Trust

The sheriff had consoled Kathleen through her sobbing. She was still terribly afraid for her son's safety but she had fought through the tears for the time being. Each of them had said all they could about Tyler and everything that was going on around him and now they were stuck playing the waiting game. Unfortunately, Tom Petty was right, the waiting really is the hardest part.

The two of them were now sitting at the kitchen table in complete silence, his right hand holding her left and resting on the table. The sheriff had to wonder if it was wrong for him to be enjoying the holding of Kathleen's hand during such a crisis. He just couldn't help but feel appreciative of a moment that, in his heart, was a long time coming. Plus, she truly seemed to welcome the comfort and that made him feel good, too.

It was a significant moment in their relationship. It had

launched their emotional connection forward by leaps and bounds. There had always been a connection. The sheriff would be the first to admit that it had been there from the very beginning. But, Kathleen was finally in a place in her life where she would admit it, too. And, that connection had grown over the years but it had done so at about the same pace as the cliff-growing white cedar trees in the Great Lakes region that are more than one hundred and fifty years old and only four inches tall.

Then, Tyler was in the car accident and the sheriff was so great through the whole event that Kathleen finally invited him over for dinner. This resulted in their relationship hitting a bit of a growth spurt more like a red pine tree which grows as much as two feet per year.

But, tonight, with this crisis reaching a critical point, they had experienced a new level of intimate friendship. They both knew it was heading for true romance down the road. If they could find the time to focus on it, they knew it had the potential of becoming more like bamboo, which shoots up as much as four inches in a day.

There was no sign of ever turning back. They both loved the idea of what the future could look like for them. But, for now, it would go unspoken. Tonight, the attention needed to remain on Tyler's future. And, that future began now. But, Kathleen and the sheriff were stuck playing that awful waiting game to find out if

Tyler was presently safe and sound.

As a result, Kathleen nearly jumped out of her skin when the phone rang. She immediately rushed over to it, not taking even a split second to re-compose herself. She had the phone against her ear before the first ring had finished. "Tyler?" she asked, contradictorily filled with equal parts hope and fear. She anxiously adjusted the phone against her ear like she would somehow be able to get it closer and hear him if his voice was faint.

"Hi, mom" Tyler said on the other end, feeling ashamed of the fact that he left her hanging for so long.

"Oh, thank God!" she exclaimed before immediately inquiring, "Are you okay?"

"I'm fine," he reassured her. "I'm sorry for worrying you."

"You should be," she quickly retorted.

"I already said I am."

"That doesn't mean we won't talk about it later. Now, where are you?"

"Jessie's."

"Good."

"I didn't know where else to go. You'll never believe the night I've had."

"Sheriff Wilson's here. He told me all about it. And, I told him all about you, too."

"You what?" Tyler asked. He was shocked by her confession, particularly after their prior agreement not to tell anyone. "Mom…" Tyler stopped his sentence and, instead, mouthed the words *My mom told Sheriff Wilson* to Jessie.

Jessie mouthed back the words *It's going to be okay* without hesitating.

Tyler believed her and it felt good.

"He wants to help," Kathleen told him.

"I'm sure he does," Tyler acknowledged. "I just… The more people that know the more scared I get."

"That's why you told Preston?" she countered.

The sheriff mouthed the words *I'll go get him* to Kathleen who responded by mouthing the words *I'll go with you.*

"That was a mistake," Tyler admitted to his mom through the phone.

The sheriff mouthed the words *If anyone's looking for him, it'll be less obvious if I do it myself.*

Kathleen reluctantly shrugged her shoulders, caving in, and the sheriff started gathering his things to go.

"Did you tell Jessie?" Kathleen asked, turning her attention back to her son.

"Yeah, but…"

"It's okay," Kathleen said, surprising her son. "I think that's the right circle of trust. But, it can't get any bigger. We won't tell anyone else. Agreed?"

"Agreed," he responded conclusively. "For reals this time."

"Absolutely. Sheriff Wilson is going to go and pick you up. He'll keep you safe and the two of you can talk on your way back here."

"Do you really think I should come back to the house?"

"I do," she answered decisively.

Tyler took a deep breath and exhaled a massive sigh of exasperation. He didn't know what to do so he decided to just trust his mom. "Okay," he finally settled.

"He's already on his way," Kathleen assured her son as the sheriff walked out the door and shut it behind him.

"Alright," Tyler responded. "I'll see you in a bit."

"Oh…" Kathleen started. She felt like she wanted to reach through the phone and hold on to her son. It came from a desire to keep him safe and make herself feel better. "I don't know if I can hang up the phone," Kathleen admitted.

"Mom," Tyler said with a hint of embarrassment as if Jessie could hear his mom babying him. "I'll be home soon and I should say goodbye to Jessie before the sheriff gets here."

"Okay. You're right. Bye, Sweetie."

"Bye," Tyler said as he nervously hung up the phone.

Kathleen listened to Tyler hang up. She lowered the phone from her ear and held it in front of her, looking at it anxiously.

Finally, she sighed as she hung up and began to cry again. This was a calmer cry but the emotion was just as deep. She knew that Tyler was safe but there was no guarantee he would stay that way. The future was too uncertain for her to find comfort. Nothing was more important to her than Tyler and the thought of anything taking him away from her was enough to send her into hysterics. She had finally heard from Tyler and he was both safe and sound. That's exactly what she wanted but the fear still wasn't gone. She just couldn't shake it. At this moment, she was unable to convince herself that she would ever be able to.

Back at Jessie's house, Tyler looked at the girl he adored with all of his heart. Just standing there with her would typically make him beam with joy. But, right now, he was afraid just like his mom. "My life is never going to be normal again, is it?"

"Probably not," Jessie answered honestly. She smiled a comforting smile and then reassured him, "But who wants normal?"

CHAPTER THIRTY-FIVE
Guardians

From inside the police cruiser, as it pulled away from the curb, Tyler exchanged a wave with Jessie who was back in her bedroom and watching from the window.

"So," the sheriff began to ask, "how long have you been interested in Jessie?"

"Just about my whole life," Tyler responded as he peeled his eyes away from the passenger side window to glance at the sheriff and around the vehicle before turning his attention to the road. He had never been inside a police car before and briefly thought about the fact that he was sitting in the passenger seat. He wondered what it would be like to ride in the back and immediately hoped he would never have to find out.

"I know the feeling," the sheriff insisted with a playful chuckle that interrupted Tyler's train of thought.

"I guess you do," Tyler said as he looked back at the sheriff

223

again with a smile. The two of them had a lot more in common than either of them had ever realized. The bonding had started over Washington-bred music that had been popular over the last half of a century. This newfound bond, regarding the years each had spent not-so-secretly pining away for a girl who seemed out of their reach, had immediately thrown the relationship into wet cement. Add to that the fact that the sheriff was one of only three people who weren't family but knew about Tyler and the cement was already hardening. Once again, they each silently appreciated the moment.

Leaving the neighborhood, the sheriff drove across the main road and pulled the cruiser into a convenience store parking lot. "I'm just going to grab a pack of cigarettes real quick," he told Tyler as he parked and turned the engine off.

"You smoke?" Tyler asked, surprised.

"Not in a really long time," the sheriff admitted. "But, I've been wanting one real bad for a couple of days now. Don't tell your mom, okay?"

"Why? You guys finally a couple?"

"Not yet. But, I hope the relationship train's heading in that direction and I'd rather not let one little slip up derail it."

"And, I know that feeling," Tyler said as the two shared a knowing grin.

"You need anything?"

"I'm good."

Tyler watched the sheriff climb out of the car and then poke his head back in before closing the door. "Would that be okay with you? Your mom and me?"

Tyler nodded affirmatively. "Absolutely," he assured the sheriff with a smile.

"Good," the sheriff said as the smile became contagious. He knocked on the roof of his car as if the relief he felt had to express itself somehow. Pulling his head back out of the car, the sheriff stood up straight. Between his evening with Kathleen and this car ride with Tyler, he suddenly felt taller than he had in a long time.

As the sheriff started to shut the door, Tyler wondered to himself if this moment was a glimpse of what it would have been like to have a father around as he grew up. The process was interrupted when a robber sprinted out of the store with a plastic bag full of money and his gun drawn.

In one fluid, instantaneous motion, the sheriff released the door and instinctively drew the gun from his holster. "Freeze!" he yelled at the robber who stopped in his tracks for only a split second. His eyes were bugging out as he realized the severity of his bad luck in having the sheriff pull into the parking lot at the end of his robbery. He continued to run, turning up the street and away from the sheriff. "Oh, come on," the sheriff said to himself before glancing back down at Tyler and holstering his gun. "Stay here!" he yelled as he started to run after the robber.

Tyler watched from inside the car, his heart beginning to gallop, as the sheriff disappeared from view. He hesitated for a moment, thinking about the fact that the sheriff was risking a lot to help him. He owed the sheriff the same kind of loyalty if they were going to be a team. And, it felt like this part of what the sheriff had referred to as the "relationship train" was heading in exactly that direction. Finally, he stepped out of the car, exhaled as he shut the door behind him, and inhaled deeply as he began to chase after them.

The robber turned down an alley and came to a stop in front of a tall wooden fence. The sheriff turned down the same alley and spotted him, quickly stopping to draw his gun to take aim again.

"Hold it right there!" the sheriff yelled at the robber who looked back at him, panicked, and immediately began to climb a fire escape. "Doggone this guy," the sheriff said to himself as he once again holstered his gun and chased the robber up the fire escape.

Tyler entered the alley at the same time as the robber reached the roof. So far unnoticed, Tyler immediately spotted the sheriff and rushed to follow him up the cold, metal rungs.

Sheriff Wilson reached the top of the fire escape and was instantly greeted with a boot in the face, kicking him like his head was a soccer ball. He released his grip on the railing and fell straight backward.

Tyler saw the sheriff fall and released his right hand, swinging his body out with his left, and caught the sheriff in mid-air. "You okay?" Tyler asked the sheriff.

"Are you?" the sheriff asked in response.

"Grab the ladder."

The sheriff did as instructed. "Got it," he told Tyler who let go of the sheriff and started to climb again.

Tyler reached the roof and was promptly met with gunfire.

"Tyler!" the sheriff yelled in angst. "Stay down and let me pass you!"

Ignoring the sheriff, Tyler leapt off of the fire escape and onto the roof while telekinetically redirecting the oncoming bullets and knocking the gun out of the robber's hand – all in one seamless action.

"What the…?" The robber began to ask.

Tyler interrupted the robber by continuing to use telekinesis to control the robber's own hands. Using them to make the man beat himself up by repeatedly slapping his own face with one hand and then the other, Tyler beat the man until his skin was bright red, his whole head throbbed, and he was so confused he couldn't think straight. Finally, Tyler released the robber's hands and his arms fell limply to his sides. Exhausted, the robber tried to shake off his self-administered beating. He began to stand and lunge toward Tyler but Tyler telekinetically lifted the man off of the ground and began to choke the man like Darth Vader to an Imperial Commander. He knew this wasn't the way he wanted to use his abilities but, he also knew he had to protect the sheriff and himself.

The sheriff reached the top of the fire escape again and stepped onto the roof in a bit of shock. Snapping out of it, he realized that Tyler was about to choke the life out of this criminal. He walked over to Tyler and placed a hand on his shoulder. "Let him go," the sheriff said. "Let him go, Tyler. It's over."

Tyler finally released his telekinetic grip and the robber dropped to the ground where he struggled to find his breath.

"Go on down to the car," the sheriff told Tyler as he handcuffed the robber and collected his gun. "I'll meet you there. Go."

"What just happened?" The robber was squealing through his attempts to find his breath. "Who is that kid?"

Tyler quietly turned around and walked away, leaving the sheriff both thankful and stunned. Tyler, on the other hand, felt a combination of both guilt and the fear of being discovered beginning to resurface.

CHAPTER THIRTY-SIX
Whistle-Blown

No one slept that night and morning had already arrived. Kathleen, the sheriff and Tyler were sitting at the kitchen table drinking coffee and the sheriff had just finished recounting the robbery event for Kathleen who didn't know if she should be horrified or proud.

"I'm supposed to be protecting him but there we were…" the sheriff said in disbelief.

"Crazy," Kathleen thought out loud. "What happened to the guy?"

"Frank Burg," the sheriff answered her. "From Thorp. We dropped him at the cop shop and had him booked on the way back here. That's what took so long. First run-in I've had with him but it's far from his first run-in with the law. Record's a couple of pages long. Some pretty violent stuff, too. He's going away for a long time this go round."

"Good riddance then," Kathleen chimed in.

"Absolutely," the sheriff agreed as he noticed the time. "I should probably let you two go get some sleep."

"I'm not tired," Tyler responded as the sheriff stood up from his chair.

"How are you not…?" the sheriff started to ask and then remembered who he was talking to. "Right."

"Well I sure am," Kathleen countered, "but I have to be at work in just over an hour."

Tyler suddenly heard a noise coming from in front of the house and turned his head, curious. The sheriff noticed this and asked, "What is it, Tyler?"

"Nothing, really. I just thought I heard something outside."

"I'll check on my way out," the sheriff assured them both.

"Thanks for your help Ron," Kathleen said, appreciatively.

"Yeah," Tyler agreed. "Thanks, Sheriff."

"You bet," the sheriff replied as he heard a noise that was louder than the first one. "Even I heard that."

The noise the sheriff heard was followed by additional sounds. First, it was several car doors closing and then the shuffling of feet coming up the driveway. Nerves began to rise up inside of Kathleen and Tyler. Even the sheriff showed a cautious curiosity. What at first sounded like a few people began to multiply into the chaotic sound of a whole herd. If nerves were athletic, this would be the Olympics.

"Well," the sheriff said as he approached the door, "I guess I'd better see what this is." The sheriff opened the door as if he was planning to leave and was instantaneously bombarded by reporters. He stopped in his tracks and closed the door in front of him. The sheriff turned around to face Tyler and Kathleen who were both panic stricken. "I'll handle this," he told them before opening the door again and stepping outside.

"Sheriff," a reporter asked as the sheriff closed the door behind him, "is it true that a man set to be amputated this morning was healed last night?"

"I heard that a twelve year old leukemia patient with one week left to live suddenly shows no signs of ever having had the disease at all," another reporter added. "Can you comment?"

"What do you think about the theory that Tyler Hirsch is somehow related to what happened this week in both Tokyo and Santiago?" a third reporter asked.

Amidst the chaotic barrage of questions, Sheriff Wilson finally managed to quiet the reporters down so he could speak. "Listen! This is private property and you all have thirty seconds to get off before I personally call my friend Judge Albert Watson and quickly obtain a restraining order that will keep each and every one of you outside of Penuel city limits for the rest of your natural lives. Thank you and have a nice day."

The sheriff opened the door and went back inside as the reporters hurried off the property and back onto the sidewalk while waving their arms and shouting their protests. With the door now closed behind him, the sheriff sighed deeply before commenting. "That should get them as far as the sidewalk, but you won't be able to hide from them forever." He took a minute to think back on the questions the reporters were asking and decided to probe Tyler about one of them. "Tyler, one of the reporters just tried to link you to Tokyo and Santiago."

"That's ridiculous," Tyler responded. "I've been here the whole time."

"Of course," the sheriff agreed. "But, what if this isn't happening to just you?"

As the three of them exchanged quizzical looks, there was a knock at the door. The sheriff spun around and opened it, angry. "I already told you…" He was stopped mid-sentence by the sight of two men in suits standing on the porch with their Federal Bureau of Investigation badges and identification cards already open and available for viewing.

Memories of TV shows and movies, where government agents come to the door and take aliens away to be tested in a lab, flashed through both Tyler and Kathleen's minds. These were the same thoughts they had experienced when Sheriff Wilson knocked on the door the night Kathleen had invited him over for dinner. Thankfully, now that the government agents were really here, they had him there to handle it.

"I'm agent Howard and this is agent Todd," Agent Howard said with authority. "We're with the F.B.I. and we would like to speak with Tyler Hirsch, ask him a few questions."

"Do you have a warrant?" the sheriff asked so quickly it was almost on top of agent Howard's sentence. It was also said with the authority only someone in Sheriff Ron Wilson's position could have. Of course, it helped that he was confident he knew the answer.

"No one is being arrested," Agent Howard responded with a hint of disdain for the small town sheriff.

"Then I suggest you follow the press off of this property immediately," the sheriff said, happy to have gotten the answer he expected.

"With all due respect, Sheriff, we're the F.B.I."

"I heard you the first time, but it's going to take more than a fancy badge, a Men's Warehouse special, and some gas station sunglasses to get through this door. Do I need to repeat *myself?*"

"We'll be back," Agent Howard told the sheriff.

"I'll be waiting," the sheriff said before he shut the door and turned to face Kathleen and Tyler, full of energy. "We don't have a lot of time. I have a friend who's a spook. He could change your identities…"

"Woah, woah, woah," Tyler snapped. "I'm not going anywhere and what, in the world, is a spook?"

"Sorry," the sheriff replied. "He's C.I.A., Tyler. And, you're running out of options here. These people want to turn you into a lab rat."

"They can't," Tyler said as he tried to fight off his worst fears.

"Can and will."

"I haven't done anything wrong."

"Doesn't matter."

"It matters to me," Tyler insisted as he stormed off toward his bedroom. "I didn't ask for any of this."

"Where're you going?" Kathleen inquired.

"School," Tyler shouted from his bedroom.

"Not today, you're not."

"Why not?" Tyler asked as he walked back into the room with a coat in his hand.

"They'll be watching you," the sheriff interjected.

"So, let 'em watch."

"Just stay home today," the sheriff suggested. "It'll give us all twenty-four hours to think about it."

"Fine," Tyler said as he stormed back off to his room, feeling frustrated about the injustice of it all. Had he given it a little bit of thought, he probably would have realized that, like the moment just before the robber stormed out of the convenience store, this too was a snapshot of what it would have been like to have a father growing up.

Unfortunately for all three of them, things would have to get worse before they even stood a chance of getting better.

CHAPTER THIRTY-SEVEN
Musketeers

Like everyone else with full knowledge of Tyler's circumstance, Jessie had been awake all night. She couldn't stop thinking about Tyler and what he was going through. She felt both sad and thrilled for him. She was mostly optimistic about the great possibilities that it presented. However, she also couldn't ignore Tyler's fear of being taken away and studied in a lab somewhere. Or, even worse, being killed out of humanity's common fear of what they don't know and understand. She knew those concerns were just as valid. As a result, there was no arguing the importance of keeping a lid on the whole thing.

More importantly, however, Jessie was just glad to have Tyler back in her life after missing his friendship for so long. He had always been such a good person. Even as a little kid, he was the moral compass in their trio. She reflected on a time they were playing a version of Swiss Family Robinson in the woods behind

Preston's house. They couldn't have been more than eight years old. They found a stack of at least twenty nasty magazines someone had stuffed in a plastic grocery bag and hidden inside of a hollowed out stump. Preston, of course, wanted to take them to school and sell them at a premium. Jessie, being a more timid child and probably in a bit of shock because she had never seen anything quite like them, was quiet on the subject. Tyler didn't even try to argue with Preston. He nearly started a forest fire when he pulled a lighter out of his pocket and set the large stack of magazines ablaze. Tyler simply held Jessie's hand and watched them burn with a smile on his face, knowing that he'd done the right thing. Preston, on the other hand, was completely livid as he tried to put the fire out but was unable to do so. The magazines had gone up in flames like they'd been doused in gasoline. By the time the fire was finally out there was nothing left but black ashes that the light breeze had already begun to scatter around their forested playground.

Jessie beamed as she reflected on Tyler's contagious smile and realized that he was virtually incorruptible. In her mind, the fact that Tyler had healed Graham after Graham caused that car accident was proof that the sweet little boy she had grown up with hadn't changed much and that abilities like these couldn't possibly be in better hands.

Between classes, she saw Preston at his locker, and

approached him with the intention of fulfilling her pledge to Tyler that she would make sure the dangling hemorrhoid kept his mouth shut about Tyler's situation. "I need to talk to you," she announced.

"About what, your highness?" Preston asked without looking, having recognized her voice. The resentment he felt toward her immediately surfaced in his unmistakably bitter tone. "Forgive me for not bowing, by the way. Hands are full, you know."

Ignoring his snarky comment, Jessie started right in. "People are beginning to find out about Tyler and if I find out you aren't keeping your mouth shut…"

"Finding out about Ty…" Jessie now had Preston's full attention. He spun around with his face displaying the encumbrance of his surprise. "Woah… How do you know… What do you know about Tyler?"

"He told me everything," she said bluntly. "And, he told me you know, too. So, I don't think we need to say it out loud. Although, I hear you've already done a bit of that which is totally uncool, by the way."

"He told you?"

"Yes, he did. And, if anyone else finds out about it I'm coming after you."

"I've already gotten this speech from Tyler and, quite frankly,

I think we both know why he scares me a lot more than you do."

"If you don't keep your mouth shut, my wrath will be so furious you'll be begging for Tyler's," the once timid girl blurted out as she stood firm without so much as a flinch in her eyes. She took a deep breath. Clearly, she hadn't finished saying her peace yet. "I want to go on record right now as saying that you're not the friend to Tyler that you've pretended to be for all of these years. I cannot believe the way you tried to exploit him."

This struck two nerves with Preston. She was right about the exploitation and he was already carrying a ton of guilt in his heart over that. But, the other nerve that it struck was one that he could fight back on and he let her have it on that one. "Man, are you ever audacious, Princess. I may have made a mistake but your track record is appalling. Why do you suddenly care?"

"I've always cared," Jessie insisted.

"No. Don't give me that line. It's unacceptable. That guy's been in love with you his whole life and you haven't said more than *hi* to him since sixth grade. How is that caring?"

"In love with…" Jessie was truly taken aback. "What are you talking about?"

"Oh, come on. No one is that dense. Everyone else sees it. Don't pretend you don't, because I'm not buying it. Even your dumb jock boyfriend with his head full of Velveeta sees it. You think Graham honestly can't remember Tyler's name? He purposely demeans my boy because he's threatened by him. Tyler's been in love with you since before he was old enough to know what he was feeling. Why do you think when we played all of those stupid tree fort games in the woods he always wanted to be the dad and you were the mom. I got stuck being some lame kid unless I insisted on being a native that you guys had befriended. The point is, he's loved you almost his whole life. But you've spent the last six or seven years ignoring him because someone with a higher social status, in spite of being one can of Rotel short of a delicious queso dip, was willing to pay you half the attention that he was."

"I honestly…" Jessie tried to respond but couldn't find the words. Tears flooded toward the front of her eyes and she silently begged herself to hold them back from overflowing.

"Maybe you are telling the truth," Preston admitted while he shut his locker and locked it. "Maybe you're so dense that you really couldn't tell. Or, maybe it's not even a matter of being dense. Maybe it was just too hard to see what was going on in the cheap seats from the Presidential suite. Either way, I'm a better friend to him than you'll ever be."

Jessie was left searching for a place to hide so she could cry in private as Preston stormed away. *Have I really been that blind?* she wondered as she practically leapt forward, opened a janitor's closet, and closed the door behind her like a child hiding from the boogey man. She immediately began to sob harder in that dark closet full of cleaning supplies than she could remember ever having sobbed before.

CHAPTER THIRTY-EIGHT
Table For Four At Hirsch's

Kathleen was in the kitchen, finally preparing the oven-roasted pork with potatoes, carrots and onions that she had offered to the sheriff a couple of nights earlier. Tyler and the sheriff were sitting in the living room watching the Mariners play the Angels on TV and cheering as Ken Griffey, Jr. belted a home run out of the park.

"My, oh my!" Mariners announcer Dave Niehaus' voice emanated from the television. "Goodbye, baseball!"

"I think he might have launched that thing into orbit," Tyler yelled enthusiastically as he and the sheriff both got so excited that their voices drowned out the announcers.

"That ball's never going to be found," the sheriff proclaimed.

What'd I miss," Kathleen said as she rushed into the room to see what the excitement was all about.

At the same time, Tyler suddenly went silent. He had turned

his attention to the front door after hearing footsteps in the driveway that sounded like they were getting closer to the house.

"Junior's two-run homer puts the M's up by one," the sheriff enthusiastically told Kathleen. They were so entranced in the baseball game that they didn't even notice anything going on with Tyler until he abruptly opened the door to see who it was.

"Tyler, what are you doing?" the sheriff asked a little too late.

"Hey," Tyler said, relieved as he saw Jessie walking up the steps to the front door.

"Hey," she responded. "Did you know there are people camping out on your sidewalk?"

Looking out at the press on the sidewalk, Tyler also noticed the government agents doing their surveillance from a parked sedan. "Yeah," he answered. "Pretty weird, right?"

"No," she responded, sarcastically. "I'm used to the paparazzi. No biggie."

"Popularity hazard?"

"Totally."

"Invite her in," Kathleen piped up in the background. "It's dinner time."

Embarrassed, Tyler closed his eyes and shook his head with a little chuckle before looking back at Jessie. "Hungry?"

Jessie smiled warmly, "I am."

Tyler was pleasantly surprised that she wanted to stay for

dinner. He closed the door behind her as she stepped inside.

Kathleen pulled the casserole dish out of the oven, sliced up the pork, strained the cooked vegetables, plated it all on dishes for serving and carried them over to the dinner table. Meanwhile, Jessie called her parents to let them know she was going to be at Tyler's for dinner. They sounded as pleased as Kathleen was by the news.

The foursome had a delicious dinner but the main attraction was the enjoyable company. They got along famously. Kathleen served as the master of ceremonies by entertaining everyone, particularly the sheriff, with embarrassing stories of Tyler and Jessie as kids. One of the sheriff's favorites was from the day of Preston's dad's wedding. She had found Tyler, Jessie and Preston in Bill Gibson's garage only minutes before the ceremony. They were, of course, dressed to the nines but had somehow managed to cover themselves from head to toe in green paint and birdseed and looked like creatures from an old B-level science fiction movie.

After dinner, the sheriff and Kathleen sat at the table talking like they had done after their first dinner together. Jessie and Tyler went down the hallway to Tyler's bedroom. Jessie, of course, hadn't seen it in years. As Tyler sat on his bed, she looked around his room, visiting a familiar place full of fond memories.

"Your room hasn't changed much," Jessie observed.

"Different posters, newer computer… I've never seen it this clean before, that's for sure."

"I don't sleep anymore," Tyler responded. "So, I've got a lot of time on my hands. I guess there're some benefits to that."

"You used to get like ten hours a night. Even as a little kid."

"Sometimes more in high school. Especially on the weekends."

"Crazy."

"I know," he agreed.

"Are you coming to school tomorrow?" Jessie asked as she finally sat down on the bed next to Tyler.

"Yeah."

"I'm going to tell Graham it's over between us."

"You are?"

"He doesn't treat me the way he should," she admitted.

"He never did."

"I know," Jessie said with a little smile that indicated she knew Tyler was the kind of guy who would treat her right. She wished she'd seen it sooner. There was a brief moment of silence in which emotions were shared between them that needed no words to convey their feelings. She leaned in to kiss him but was interrupted by the sound of the door opening.

"Oh," the sheriff let out. He was embarrassed by his own intrusion as he saw Jessie and Tyler quickly scoot apart from one another. "I'm sorry."

"No," Jessie said. "Sheriff, it's okay."

"Yeah," Tyler interjected. "We were just talking."

"Well," the sheriff said as he tried to move on from the embarrassment of having clearly broken up a moment, "I'm leaving so, I just wanted to say goodbye."

"Okay," Tyler said. "Thanks for coming over."

"Sure. I'll probably check in on you tomorrow, too. Just to make sure everything's going alright."

"Yeah, okay."

"I'm also wondering if I shouldn't drive Jessie home so she doesn't get harassed by the press."

"She's used to it," Tyler said glancing at Jessie and sharing a chuckle at their inside joke.

"What?" the sheriff asked, confused.

"Nothing," Tyler said.

"I'd appreciate it," Jessie told the sheriff.

Jessie and Tyler followed the sheriff back to the front of the house. They said goodnight to each other and Jessie climbed into the front seat of the sheriff's patrol car. Tyler went back to his room and the sheriff stayed on the porch to say goodnight to Kathleen.

"I think I might have broken up some kind of moment in there between the kids," the sheriff said to Kathleen in a whisper.

"You're kidding," Kathleen responded with a smile that revealed she was glad to hear that they were having one.

"No, I feel sort of bad about it."

"Oh, don't worry about it. I thought you looked a little flush though."

"Probably," he admitted. "It was kind of embarrassing."

"This was fun, wasn't it? The four of us…"

"It was," the sheriff agreed. "Why don't you let me take you out for a dinner tomorrow. You know, in a restaurant so you don't have to cook. All four of us if you'd like."

"Tomorrow is Friday. That's graduation, assuming it's okay to let Tyler go. You could come with me. I'm sure Tyler would like it if you were there."

"I'd like that, too. But, I think you're a week early. Graduation is next Friday, isn't it?"

"Oh, gosh. You're right. My mind is so scattered right now."

"Understandable, considering the circumstances."

"Thanks," Kathleen said, still a bit embarrassed. "It's a date."

"It's two dates."

"Even better," she said with a smile. She leaned forward and kissed the sheriff on the cheek. "Goodnight, Ron."

"Goodnight," the sheriff responded with an uncontrollable smile.

Kathleen watched the sheriff walk away and waited to close

the door until the patrol car pulled out of the driveway. "Alright," she shouted to the back of the house. "How'd it go with Jessie?"

Tyler walked in the room, feigning a strut. "Let's just say between Jessie and I, and you and the sheriff, the Hirsch house is becoming quite the love shack."

Kathleen raised her hand in the air and exchanged a high five with her son before they walked to the kitchen to clean up from a very successful dinner.

CHAPTER THIRTY-NINE
Breakfast Tornado

Kathleen was trying to put on an earring while scanning the inside of the refrigerator for eggs and bacon. As she finally got the back onto her earring, she realized that there were no eggs and there was no bacon to be found. So, after a brief sigh, she simply grabbed the orange juice carton and set it on the counter before taking her foot off of the bottom corner of the refrigerator door and allowing it to close itself.

She spun around, popped open a cupboard door and put her other earring in while looking for instant oatmeal. With both earrings now in, she rearranged a few items and finally found what she was looking for, the rectangular box with the guy in the funny hat on the front. Kathleen pulled the box out before opening yet another cupboard door and reaching inside to remove a small drinking glass as Tyler walked by looking ready for school.

"Where're you going?" she asked as she filled the glass with water and put it in the microwave.

"I'll give you a hint," he started.

"If you're about to remind me that it's a school day, I assure you there is no need. I work at a bank. We have very similar hours. In fact, your schedule is why I started working at a bank in the first place. So, the next question is, are you sure that's a good idea?" Kathleen set the timer for two minutes and hit the start button before turning around to face her son.

"Are you sure it's not?"

"Sit down. I'm making oatmeal. Have you seen the news this morning?"

"I don't have time for oatmeal and no, I haven't really wanted to watch the news lately. Why?"

"It's instant oatmeal. There's always time. And, the news is about another miracle. This one happened in Helsinki."

"Finland?"

"An outbreak of massive tornadoes. People are claiming to have seen a young woman reach up to the sky like she was calling on them. Apparently, their funnels all collapsed vertically up into the sky. Then they grouped together like they were forming one super tornado before reaching back down. They suddenly took her up into the sky and she immediately disappeared with the storms. It all just vanished in the blink of an eye. City saved."

"I have to admit, that does sound pretty amazing."

"I'm terrified by the fact that, in all of these miraculous events around the world, the people performing those miracles have been taken away at the end of it. What if you're next? What if I'm about to lose you?"

Tyler watched as his mom lost the fight to hold back her tears. He didn't have the answer but he knew he needed to try and offer some comfort. He wasn't about to make something up and lie to his mom. But, he knew he had to offer some hope for a mother who might be on the verge of losing her son. Tyler searched for something and finally said, "First of all, that assumes these things are related."

"Well, a lot of people think these other three things are related and you know full well some people have already roped you in with them. Are you saying they're wrong?"

"I'm not saying anything other than we don't know. And, besides, assuming all four of us are somehow tied together, what if my miracle came and went at the hospital and I'm still here?" Tyler was sure he had just given his mother the hope she needed. He watched her, expecting her expression to change to reflect her encouragement. Unfortunately, he didn't have to wait long to discover that, that wasn't going to happen.

"For some reason, I don't think you're done."

Tyler thought about his mom's reaction. He didn't know if

she was right to worry or if that was just a waste of energy. She was right, of course, that when you considered the other big miracles that had happened recently, there was plenty to be concerned about. But, even though she might be right that he was connected to these events, they simply couldn't be sure one way or the other. He was also confident that worrying would not help any of it at all. What he did know with absolute certainty was that he just wanted to be able to live his life, however much of it had changed and regardless of how short it may now be cut. Unfortunately, he couldn't help but catch a bit of the sadness virus from his mom. "You're making it sound like a destiny thing. Unavoidable."

"If that woman from twenty-five years ago was right, that's exactly what it is. I thought she was nuts back then. Now, I'm inclined to believe her."

"If it's destiny then staying home isn't going to keep me from it."

"No, I suppose not," Kathleen conceded as the microwave beeped to indicate the two minute zap was complete. She got a bowl out from a cupboard, tore open a little brown packet of oatmeal and emptied the contents into the bowl.

Tyler was finally convinced that he couldn't really offer anything that comforted his mom and it frustrated him to the point where he was feeling antsy. The silence of the moment was driving him crazy, too. Luckily, his mom finally broke it.

"Look," she said, "I don't have time to argue with you about this."

"Good. Then don't. I need to get out of here anyway."

"Come straight home after school. When I get home from work, we're going to sit down with Ron and talk about what to do next."

"Fine."

"Are you walking?" she asked.

"I don't have a car and I'm not speaking to Preston. So, the options are pretty limited."

"I can drive you. How's that for another option?"

"You'll be late for work."

"Not if I skip my oatmeal."

"Eat your oatmeal. I can walk."

"Then you'll be late."

"I'm pretty sure tardy has less consequence in high school than it does at work and I know it's less frowned upon than total absence so, I'd better get going."

"What about the people outside?"

"I'll figure out a way around them."

"Just be careful."

"I think we both know I can take care of myself."

"You know the number at the bank just in case, right?"

"For more than a decade now."

"Okay," Kathleen said as she walked over and gave her son a hug. She was trying hard not to overstate her concern but, the truth was, she was completely terrified over all of this and Tyler was well aware of it. There simply was no way to protect her son's wellbeing when something was clearly going on that was far bigger than any of the people involved.

"Bye, mom."

"I'll see you tonight," she said as she planted a kiss on his cheek and then quickly wiped a tear away from her own.

Tyler let go of his mom and headed out the back door. He snuck into the backyard and disappeared into the woods, leaving his mom with no control, no real reassurance, and nothing to do but continue worrying. A reminder beep from the microwave startled her a bit. She opened the door, took out the glass, and poured the water over her oatmeal before setting the glass down on the counter next to the carton of orange juice. She opened a drawer, pulled out a spoon and started stirring her breakfast.

Kathleen didn't even notice when she had stopped stirring. It was as if her body, mind and soul had joined together to convince her that there was only one thing to do. So, in an act of obedience, she just closed her eyes and began to pray.

CHAPTER FORTY
Relationship Jumble

Tyler pushed open the front door to the high school and walked inside. He was not surprised to see that the gossip circus was back in town. To make matters worse, it appeared that he was still the unwitting star of their silly little show. His tummy felt like it was doing a solo high-flying trapeze act without a net. He attempted to focus on trying to live his life and do his best to keep the circus from bothering him any more than was inevitable. As the stares and whispers continued, it became obvious that this would be a task easier said than done. Although any distraction would seem to be welcome, an unwelcome one presented itself within ten seconds of entering the building. It came in the form of Preston who vigorously approached him.

"Tyler," Preston said expectantly, as he caught up with him and spun around to walk with him. He kept pace with Tyler who ignored him as he walked with no change either in his pace or in the expression on his face. After waiting for a response that clearly wasn't coming, Preston tried again. "Tyler!"

"What?" Tyler finally reacted as he stopped in his tracks but still refused to look him in the face. The few people who weren't already watching Tyler turned to see what the commotion was about.

"I need to talk to you."

"Too bad, Preston. Because, I'm not ready to talk to you. I have nothing to say right now. And, frankly, I'm not sure when or even if I ever will."

"Come on, man. I'm really wigging out about this. I went totally Professor Brainard over the greenback and I just need you to let me apologize. I really did want to help but I know I was a total fetus and I couldn't possibly be any more sorry."

Tyler finally turned and looked Preston in the eyes. "You should be," he said without shouting but so forcefully he felt like he might burst a vein in his forehead. He took a moment to compose himself before speaking again. "I trusted you," he finally said before turning away again. As he started to walk away he muttered, "I can't do this right now."

Preston stood in the hallway, distraught and feeling utterly alone in a building filled with people. He quickly realized that those people were still staring at him and reacted by trying to play it cool with an announcement, "Show's over folks." People kept talking about the commotion as they began to turn away. Preston looked around and spotted Tyler approaching Jessie at her locker as if there were no longer any bad blood between them. This felt like the proverbial salt on the wound and made him feel absolutely devastated. He turned and walked in the opposite direction. "Show's most definitely over."

"How's it goin'?" Tyler asked Jessie as he leaned against a neighboring locker.

"Fantastic," Jessie responded, lighting up. "How are you?"

"Not too bad. It's nice to finally be out of the house."

"I'll bet."

"Although, I could do without running into Preston."

"Story of my life."

"Yeah, true. I think I finally get it. I could also do without all of the strange looks and constant whispering."

"Now, see, that I don't quite get."

"Really? I thought with all of your paparazzi experience…"

"Funny but, no. I mean it. You need to be a little more realistic about this."

"Careful. You're starting to sound like Preston.

"That can't be good. But, what I mean is, can you really blame them for staring and for all of the chatter? I saw on the news when I got home last night that some of the people you healed in the hospital were only days away from death. People with cancer, AIDS… It's just so… It's incredible. Of course people are looking at you. Of course people are talking about you. You did something amazing, Tyler. You should be proud of yourself," she told him as she placed her hand on his arm, emphasizing her point.

Tyler felt his body heat up at her touch. This was a completely different sensation than the kind of heat he felt when he healed someone. Having never really dated because he was always in love with the girl whose hand was now on his arm, it was a sensation he had never felt before. He didn't want to show her how much of an effect it had on him but he didn't want her to stop either. So, he decided to play it cool but flirty. He cocked his head and grinned as he asked "Amazing like, intellectually stimulating? Or, amazing like, crazy-sexy?"

"Rest assured, Tyler Hirsch, those two things are not mutually exclusive," Jessie said with a huge, flirtatious smile of her own.

"That's good to hear because I'm finding myself to be a heck of a lot more intelligent since this all started happening," Tyler expressed as he inched closer to her.

"Really?" Jessie responded, as if her level of intrigue had just increased.

"Absolutely," Tyler flirtatiously reassured her.

Anyone who didn't know better would have watched and

thought they had been a couple for a long time. Perhaps it had something to do with the fact that Tyler had been in love with Jessie for most of his life. Perhaps it was equally critical to the equation that deep down, Jessie had also been in love with Tyler for most of hers and was finally allowing those feelings to surface. All of the onlookers in the hallway were watching Tyler but felt that what they were currently witnessing was something very new. The pair gave the gossip circus exactly what it wanted. With the exit of Preston complete, Jessie was now the new co-star in this show.

As if the show needed more drama, another character quickly entered the scene. Graham appeared, seemingly out of nowhere, having obviously been one of the witnesses to their newborn closeness. Graham had spent his time in the hospital unsure of how to respond to Tyler when he saw him next. There was no question that he was scared, but he didn't know if he should admit it by suddenly being nice to him. Seeing him with Jessie put that question to its final resting place as his emotions got the best of him.

"What's goin' on here, freak?" he asked, crossly. His angry voice startled both Tyler and Jessie which, to Tyler's dismay, caused the warm moment of Jessie's hand on Tyler's arm to come to an abrupt end. "You hittin' on my girl now that you think you're some kind of a hero? I know better. Don't I, freak?"

"Alright," Jessie started as she stepped in front of Graham and his goon-squad. "Welcome back to school, Graham. You and I need to talk."

"Jessie…" Tyler started, protectively.

Jessie spun around to reassure Tyler she would be okay. "I'll keep it public. How does right outside of the main office sound?"

"Smart," Tyler agreed.

"I'll see you at lunch," Jessie said, warmly.

"Okay," Tyler consented as he watched her lead Graham away, catching hostile looks from both Graham and his cronies as they all exited the scene.

As if the gossip circus and concern over Jessie's meeting with Graham weren't stressful enough, Tyler soon found himself sitting alone on the opposite side of Mr. Russell's earth science classroom from Preston. Mr. Russell rambled on about Washington State's boorish, glaciated, volcanic medley of a crust that had supposedly been active for the last hundred million years. Meanwhile, Tyler noticed Preston sitting alone as well and that old familiar feeling of guilt started to set in again.

CHAPTER FORTY-ONE
Goodbye, Normal

"Is this seat taken?" Jessie asked Tyler who, until she approached him, was sitting alone at a table just outside of the cafeteria.

"Well," he answered without looking, "I was saving it for Gwen Stefani, but she didn't show up. So, I guess it's cool. Park it."

They shared a smile and Jessie sat down to eat the chicken salad that she had just purchased. "Did you notice those guys across the street?" she asked. "They're watching every move you make."

Tyler looked just beyond the school grounds and spotted the F.B.I. agents with binoculars joined to their eye sockets. "Not exactly subtle, are they?" he remarked.

"Not even a little bit," she concurred.

"So, how did it go with Graham?"

"I did it."

"Really?"

"Really."

"I'm impressed. How did he take it?"

"Not well."

"Poor guy," Tyler said with a thick layer of sarcasm.

"Poor guy? Poor girl! I'm the one that put up with his garbage for…"

"Way too long," Tyler finished for her in total agreement.

"Absolutely."

"How does it feel?"

"Liberating," Jessie said with an exaggerated sigh of relief and a smile.

"I have to admit, I feel a little of that myself."

Just like he had in the school hallway earlier, Graham appeared, seemingly out of nowhere, with his disciples in tow. "I knew you were scopin' Jessie out," Graham told Tyler before turning his attention to Jessie. "And you were just ripe for the pickin', weren't you? This was either already going on behind my back or you let this freak jump in, in less than four hours. Either way, you know what that makes you?"

"Just leave us alone," Jessie told Graham.

"It makes you a dirty little…"

"Don't even think about finishing that sentence," Tyler

directed Graham with authority.

"So the hero is back," Graham mocked. "I'll tell you what, freak. You can have her. I brought her out of the nerd-herd and I'll be happy to send her back. But, it is gonna cost you."

"Graham," Tyler instructed, "if I were you, I'd stop talking."

Graham bent down to get in Tyler's face. "Well, you're not me, are you, freak?"

"No," Tyler admitted as he stood up and stepped away from Graham. "No, I'm not. And, thank God for that."

Graham stood up to stay at Tyler's level. "Where do you think you're going? I'm not done with you."

Suddenly, every single drink in the area either pulled right out of students' hands or rose straight up from the tables. Milk cartons, juice bottles and soda cans all floated to a position just above Graham's head. The students and faculty behind Graham all watched in awe but he and his goons were so focused on Tyler that they didn't see what was going on. Tyler took another step away and Jessie got to her feet so she could follow his lead.

"I've got you right where I want you," Graham charged. "You won't do anything out here in front of all these people."

"I'm full of surprises," Tyler said just before every drink container in the area simultaneously dumped its contents on Graham and his followers. They were stunned as the variety of liquids completely drenched them.

"Get 'em both," Graham coached his allies.

"You touch Jessie and I'll make you regret it," Tyler insisted in a tone that left no question about his sincerity.

"You're bluffing," Graham retaliated.

Tyler glanced down at Graham's crotch. Then looked him confidently in the eyes again. "Try me."

The not so subtle reminder of the condition from which Tyler had healed him gave Graham brief pause. But, his anger and pride were stronger than his conscience. "Just get him!"

Mr. Russell started to rush in and stop the melee, but Mr. Brooks held him back because he wanted to see what would happen next.

Graham's disciples tried to attack Tyler, but they suddenly flipped head over feet and landed on their bellies, unable to get up because of an invisible force holding them down.

Graham panicked, grabbed a student's fork, wrapped Jessie up with the other arm and put the fork to Jessie's neck.

Tyler saw this and focused in on it. In his peripheral vision, Tyler saw Preston start to move on Graham from the crowd and he signaled him to stay put. He then released Graham's cronies and they ran away, trembling. Mr. Brooks and Mr. Russell stopped them before they could go anywhere.

Graham's hand slowly moved away from Jessie no matter how hard he tried to keep it there. Jessie was suddenly released from Graham's grip and she stepped away safely. The fork slowly moved toward Graham's neck, ultimately resting tightly against his skin.

"What the…?" Graham whimpered. "Let me go, man!"

"Why?" Tyler asked, scrupulously. "Do you deserve to be let go, Graham?" After not getting a response, Tyler insisted, "Do you?"

"No," Graham finally admitted.

"What?" Tyler persisted as he caused the fork to increase its pressure until it began to draw a small amount of blood.

"Come on," Graham sniveled. "I said no, man!"

"Why not?"

Agents Howard and Todd climbed out of their sedan and stood side-by-side, anxiously watching the action through binoculars.

"I see blood," Agent Howard announced.

"Barely," Agent Todd argued. I've cut myself worse when shaving. Besides, we can't tell for sure Hirsch is the one doing it."

"Who else would it be?" Agent Howard asked, sincerely. "And how long are we going to wait around for another opportunity?"

"Good enough for me."

"That's assault and it's all we need."

"Let's move."

Both agents tossed the binoculars into their sedan, shut the door and began to move quickly toward the action.

Tyler continued to elicit a response that hadn't come yet. "Why not, Graham?"

"Because I'm a…" Graham started to say but didn't finish.

"Because you're a what?" Tyler asked. "You're a freak?"

"I'm a freak?" Graham asked, demoralized, as the fork pressed in just a little harder. "Okay, fine. Yes, I'm a freak."

Tyler finally noticed that the government agents were rushing toward him with their guns drawn. He released Graham, who dropped to his knees in complete humiliation.

"That was your final warning, Graham."

Tyler looked at Jessie, distressed by the idea that they were at last heading in the direction he had always hoped just as it came time for him to run and hide. All he wanted was to live a normal life with Jessie by his side. Now that seemed impossible. He and Jessie shared a look that let them both know they were feeling the same sadness. He turned and began to run.

Starting with the same journey he had been on the day this all began, Tyler sprinted toward the football field with agents Todd and Howard chasing after him. He crossed the football field, climbed the chain-linked fence that surrounded it, and fled into the woods.

With trees whipping past him, Tyler occasionally looked

behind him to see if the agents were still on his trail. He couldn't seem to lose them. Suddenly, a dart zipped by his head. He looked back as several more shots were fired and quickly determined that the agents were trying to tranquilize him.

Tyler turned back around just in time to see a fallen tree in front of him. He leapt over it like an Olympic hurdler and then stopped. He turned around to face the agents and the fallen tree rose from the ground in front of him right when the agents tried to jump over it. The tree tripped them in mid-air and they fell to the ground, dropping their weapons.

Reaching his arms out in front of him, he caused the agents guns to rise up off of the ground, point back at the agents, and finally discharge. One dart hit each of the agents and they immediately became groggy. Tyler swung his arms to the right and the guns were tossed at least a hundred feet into the forest, away from the agents. He turned back around and walked away, completely alone and with no idea of where he was going or what was in store next.

CHAPTER FORTY-TWO
Collective Alarm

The sheriff had been called to the school directly following the incident between Tyler and Graham. When he had completed his initial investigation, he went straight to the bank. He drove up to the window and told Kathleen they needed to talk, that it had to do with Tyler, and that he hadn't been harmed.

Kathleen asked a co-worker to cover for her while she took a break. She and the sheriff sat in the patrol car, parked in a space on the side of the bank, discussing the incident that had occurred at the school that day. Of course, Kathleen had more questions than the sheriff had answers. But, he did his best to appease her.

Having questioned both Jessie and Preston, the worst news he had to deliver was the fact that no one knew where Tyler had gone. Kathleen was even more upset by her own inability to figure out where he would go. It was a helpless feeling. She was understandably overcome with worry for her son and it was a blessing to have the sheriff there, comforting her.

They both agreed that this was exactly what they had feared with Tyler deciding to return to school. But, focusing on that opinion would do no good now, so they agreed to let go of it and turn their focus to solving the problem rather than on how it had come about.

Clearly, Tyler was hiding out of fear and he was right to be afraid. The F.B.I. agents now had reason to take him in. The sheriff was of the opinion that the goal should be to find him and keep him hidden, even if it meant they were breaking the law by doing so. Some things are just too important, regardless of the consequences. The sheriff and Kathleen agreed, without any hesitation, that protecting Tyler was one of those things.

Kathleen left work early that day and she couldn't help but wonder if she would ever return. There was a distinct possibility that she was about to leave Penuel for a lot longer than a weekend for the first time in twenty-five years. If she did, she was fairly certain she would never come back. Whereas the idea of leaving Seattle at eighteen years old had been an exciting one, the idea of leaving Penuel at forty-three now terrified her. Of course, the circumstances had even more to do with that than her age. Twenty-five years ago she was on the hunt for a new way of life. This time around, she'd be in hiding in order to merely keep her son alive. These thoughts and the fear of not finding Tyler before the F.B.I. did, overwhelmed Kathleen as she followed the sheriff in her car on the way to her house where they intended to plan their next steps.

Meanwhile, Jessie and Preston were sharing some of the same concerns that Kathleen and the sheriff had. They were sharing theirs over a cup of coffee at a café in town called Bonnie's Mug Hug. Common distress over someone jointly cared about has a way of bonding people together. Jessie and Preston had spent a lot of time disliking one another but their love for Tyler was a firm common ground and, right now, there certainly was a lot to be distressed about. These, of course, were circumstances Jessie and Preston would do anything to reverse but, on the bright side, this was an experience that was long overdue.

"I have to admit," Jessie tossed out there, "I'm a bit skeptical."

"About me?" Preston questioned.

"Well, yeah. You haven't exactly been my biggest supporter over the years."

"Yeah," Preston conceded. "Well, first of all, ditto."

"Fair."

"And, second, I was… you know… jealous."

"Jealous?" Jessie asked, honestly surprised.

"I was," Preston admitted. "We were all on the same level

before. Tyler and I stayed there and you became the homecoming queen."

"No, I didn't. Jenny Conrad did."

"You know what I mean."

"I wasn't even the runner up."

"Oh, that's right. Virginia Leigh was. She might have won it if she'd had her work done before the vote."

Preston and Jessie shared a good laugh. The friendship was resurfacing.

"I treated you both really badly," Jessie confessed. "I'll admit that popularity has some perks but, it's totally overrated. I would love to go back and do things differently."

"Well, let's face it, we both would. Besides, I was pretty horrible to you, too. And, you didn't do anything to Tyler that was half as bad as what I did. I'm such a brown ribbon friend."

"We both are."

"Were," Preston said, suggesting a course-correction.

"Were," Jessie agreed with a smile.

"You think we'll ever see him again?"

"If I were him, I wouldn't come back."

"Me neither. I still want to find him though. I want to help him. I know he'd do it for us."

"He would," Jessie concurred. She paused the conversation as she thought about how they could find Tyler. Finally, she decided to bring Preston in on her process. "If you were him, where would you go?"

"Mexico," Preston said immediately.

"You know, if you're just trying to get out of the country, Canada's a lot closer."

"Oh, brother."

"What?"

"You two really are meant for each other."

"Who?"

"You and Tyler. He told me the same thing before this whole mess started."

"Really?" Jessie had a big smile on her face. She felt better about who she was right then, than she had in years.

In that moment, all jokes and silly comparisons aside, Preston accepted the fact that Jessie and his best friend belonged together. And, he was happy for Tyler because he knew that Tyler had dreamed about this for as long as Preston could remember. Unfortunately, Tyler wasn't there to enjoy it. It was that reality that brought everything crashing back down to earth.

Preston and Jessie talked for a bit longer before deciding to go to Tyler's house. They knew he wouldn't be there but they hoped that his mom would know what to do next. Jessie rode in Preston's Fuego for the second time that day. It was funny to her how perspectives change. On the way to the Mug Hug, she was a little grossed out by how trashy Preston's car was. But, after their time there, her perspective had changed and she realized how that crazy Fuego was a perfect fit for Preston's outrageous personality.

The ride was quiet as both of their minds drifted off in different directions but mostly landed on something that related to Tyler. One of the few times they talked was when Jessie asked Preston if they could change the rock music, that was playing just above background level, to a country station. Preston mentally cringed as he obliged and Jessie could tell he didn't want to so she put a little extra emphasis on it when she thanked him.

When they arrived at Tyler's house, they discovered that Kathleen and the sheriff had already gathered in the living room with a couple of other police officers. The six of them bundled up and took flashlights out to the woods near the high school. Each of them outwardly acted more optimistic than they truly felt as the quickly formed private search party began to scour the area for Tyler and as the sunlight slowly gave way to the darkness of night.

CHAPTER FORTY-THREE
Messengers

Tyler was completely isolated in his hillside campground. He had built a fire with his newfound abilities by using his mind to force a couple of sticks to rub together at a rapid speed that would be impossible for human hands. He stared at his main source of heat and rubbed his palms together as he thought about Chile and what had taken place there. *The entire city of Santiago was saved,* he thought. *That was an undeniable miracle.* He then thought about Finland and Japan and wondered if these events really were somehow related to what he was going through. *Those were all far more significant than anything I've done. What if my mom's right? What if there's still more left for me to do? And, what if the endgame is my death?*

Glancing around the campground, Tyler's mind began to drift to more local and less miraculous things. He thought about Preston. He remembered the times they'd shared in these very campgrounds and what good friends they'd been from such a young age. He wondered if he had overreacted to Preston's misguided attempt to get him to embrace his new abilities. Tyler sat there, all alone, with a dozen years' worth of memories flashing through his mind, and wished he'd been able to forgive Preston sooner. *I may never see him again*, he acknowledged to himself.

He began to think about everything that he feared he would never experience again. From the major to the minor. He would even miss the inane buzzing sound from the fluorescent lights in the school's hallways and classrooms when all else was silent. Or, in Tyler's case recently, every moment that he was in school whether it was noisy or not. He suddenly realized that he had heard a very similar sound in the hallways of the hospital the night he went to see Graham and wound up healing the patients in ICU. *What a silly thing to think about at a time like this*, he realized.

Tyler next thought about Jessie and how much he loved her. In all of the years that he'd had these feelings, it was the first time he'd ever allowed himself to sincerely consider the fact that what he felt toward her was a real and lasting love. Maybe he had resisted the thought in the past as a defense mechanism. Or, perhaps he just needed some reciprocation in order to be pushed over the edge into the emotional abyss that love is. Either way, he longed for the opportunity to explore it further and was afraid that the opportunity would never come.

He was glad that his mom had begun the process of grabbing a petal from the love flower, too. *The sheriff is a good man,* he thought. *That's a good fit. I hope it sticks. It's all so new to us, the sheriff and mom, Jessie and me, but I hope it can last. How could it, really? Is that even possible? What would it look like? How could anything ever be remotely normal again? Hope is the wrong word. I wish it could last.* Unfortunately, the more he considered his circumstances, the less hopeful he felt.

Before Tyler could attempt to answer any of his own questions, devise any plans, or even begin to think about how worried his mom and friends must have been about him, he looked back at the fire. What he saw scared him into jumping off of his log. He tripped and fell backwards, terrified at the sight of an elderly woman he didn't recognize but who now stood across from him on the other side of the fire.

What he didn't know was that she was the same woman who had stood in Kathleen's parents' driveway twenty-five years earlier and told her about the son she would have. And, the same woman who had stood in the grocery store and told her the time had come for the world to find out about Tyler. But, Tyler had no idea what she looked like and, therefore, he didn't recognize her or even consider that this could be the same woman.

"It's okay, Tyler," she said in a sincere attempt to comfort him. "I'm not here to harm you."

"Who are you?" Tyler asked, trepidatiously.

"I'm a messenger," she told him, matter-of-factly.

"How do you know me?" he asked, fearing the answer could have something to do with the government.

"I know the one who knew you before your mother did."

The answer gave Tyler pause. At first, he thought she could be lying to hide her true identity. But, the answer didn't make sense. Until, he slowly made the connection and began to ask, "Are you the one that my mom…?"

"I am."

Tyler got to his feet and brushed the dirt off of his jeans. "Then you must know why this is happening to me."

"I do."

"Then tell me," Tyler said as he looked up and forgot all about the dirt on his clothes. "Please, tell me."

"You're something of a messenger yourself. In a different way than me though."

Tyler's tone didn't carry the witty sarcasm he often had when talking to his mom. This was a stranger but, even more, he was just too desperate for that right now. He wanted answers and he felt like he couldn't wait another second. But, he was in no position to make demands. The best he could do was to beg. "Can you be less cryptic?"

"I'm telling you that you have a message of your own. And,

you are meant to deliver that message to the world."

"I'm really looking for specifics here," Tyler told her with an attitude that was rashly heading down the trail toward exasperation. "What's the message?"

"Everyone has a purpose, Tyler. Right now, yours is to show the world that miracles still happen."

"Why me?"

"Why not you?" she fired back at him.

"I'm nobody," he said with a hint of shame. "I'm not special."

"Ah, but you are," she disagreed. "You are special."

"I'm really not."

"You're not the first to respond this way. And, you won't be the last."

"I don't know anything about anyone else you might be referring to but I do know myself. Until quite recently, I was extremely ordinary."

"And now you know that you are as extraordinary as I've always known you to be. At times, the foolish is chosen to shame the wise and the weak is chosen to shame the strong. The when, where, who, how and why are not up to us."

"I don't understand any of that, to be perfectly honest with you."

"What's happening to you is a gift. And, by way of being the vessel of that gift, you, Tyler, are yourself a gift."

Tyler swallowed the weight of the situation. "What if I don't want this?"

"You can't change what you are," the woman said, warmly. "Oh, sure. You can run away and hide from the world. You don't have to do what you were created for. But, what a tragedy that would be. Hiding wouldn't change you. It wouldn't change who you were meant to be or, who you just flat out are. Not sharing the gift you've been given would only make your existence meaningless."

Tyler pondered the woman's statements for a moment. The size of it all was indisputable. "Does what's happening to me have anything to do with what just happened in Finland?"

The woman simply nodded affirmatively.

"Japan and Chile?" he continued to ask.

The woman's nodding continued in response to Tyler's questioning. She seemed happy to affirm for him that he wasn't the only one going through this. "You'll learn more about that later. I promise. Right now, you need to get back to where you're supposed to be. It is there that your current purpose will be fulfilled."

"My current purpose?" he asked.

"In time, Tyler. Soon. But, in time."

CHAPTER FORTY–FOUR
Strategy

The woman had disappeared in a manner Tyler should have expected from his mom's stories. Tyler had looked down, staring pensively into the fire as he thought about all he had already learned and all of the questions that he still had for her. When he looked up to ask her how he would know that his moment had come, she was gone.

He stayed at the campsite for another couple of hours. Tyler had a lot to think about. The woman had told him that hiding his gift from the world would only make his existence meaningless. He decided that this meant he somehow had to go back and live his life until his moment of destiny arrived. That's what he really wanted anyway. To live his life. To go back and spend time with Jessie. To tell Preston in person that he was forgiven. Especially now that the proverbial cat was out of the bag anyway.

What he didn't know was just how living his life was even

going to be possible now that the feds wanted to take him into custody. Had this woman given him a completely impossible task? There was only one way to find out and, ultimately, he decided to head home and figure it out on the way.

Tyler's first stop was Principal McClean's house. He had to be surreptitious about his return and every move he made along the way. So, Tyler nearly scared Principal McClean half to death when he knocked on the door in the back of his house at just after five o'clock on the Saturday morning. Tyler waited for about a minute in between knocks. Less than ten seconds after the third round of knocking, the door opened and he was greeted by a shotgun wielding principal in boxer shorts and a souvenir tank top from Sea World in San Diego, CA.

After Principal McClean got over the initial shock of seeing Tyler standing there with his hands raised, he lowered his weapon and invited Tyler inside. They had a pleasant and lengthy conversation about how to ensure that Tyler could privately take his final exams and graduate with the rest of his class. Tyler told Principal McClean how much he appreciated the help and Principal McClean wished Tyler well before sending him on his way and going back to bed with very little confidence that he'd ever get back to sleep.

The next stop for Tyler was home. He stealthily approached the property from the forest behind the house and snuck up to the back door as dawn began to push the darkness into hiding. Suspecting that there were F.B.I. agents, staked out and waiting for his arrival so they could arrest him and take him away, he was as quiet and careful as he could be.

The sliding glass door was locked but, luckily, he learned a trick with this door when he was a kid. For a long time, Jessie and Preston were the only other two that knew about it. But, a few years ago, his mom had gotten it in her head that the two of them needed to get out and exercise a little more. So, they walked to the grocery store on a sunny Saturday in the Spring. When they got home, Kathleen discovered that she had locked them out of the house. That's when Tyler finally showed her the trick he learned. It was so quick and easy, the city girl in her wanted to immediately get the locking mechanism changed. But, living in a small town had become so much a part of her that it hardly seemed necessary.

Tyler put both of his hands on the glass and pushed in and then up. He could hear the lock fall out of place. That's when he slid the door a couple of inches before letting it slowly set back into the track. He then gripped the handle as he normally would, slid it open enough for him to step inside, and then closed it behind himself and re-locked it.

Wanting to remain hidden, Tyler didn't turn any lights on. He walked quietly into the kitchen and that's when he heard the sound of a car pulling into the driveway. He peeked around the wall and saw the headlights just as they turned off and he could hear the car park and the engine turn off. He ducked back down into the kitchen and waited, nervously, as car doors opened and shut and the clip-clop sound of feet approached from the walkway in front of the house. Finally, a key hit the lock on the front door and the sound of his mom's voice reassured Tyler.

"Are you sure you don't want us to take you home?" Tyler heard his mom ask.

The only thing left to determine before he could feel completely at ease was who she had with her.

"Positive," Tyler heard Jessie say. Tyler smiled briefly but, he didn't know who the other footsteps belonged to. "We're here for the long-haul."

The door opened as Tyler wondered exactly who 'we' referred to.

"It's really nice of your parents to let you stay out all night like this," Kathleen told Jessie as they stepped inside and the door closed behind them. Kathleen flipped on the living room lights and peeled her coat off.

"They were ready to come help," Jessie insisted.

"Mine too," Preston's voice chimed in, surprising Tyler.

"Our parents love Tyler almost as much as we do, Miss Hirsch." Tyler smiled at the kind words from the girl he now knew he loved.

"That's so sweet," Kathleen said as she laid her coat on the couch. "It didn't make a lot of sense in the dark but, today's different. I'll put some coffee on and round up some breakfast while Ron calls his deputies and we can start the search again in about an hour. Maybe we can take your parents up on that offer this morning."

Before another word could be spoken, Tyler poked his head around the wall again like he had when he watched the headlights turn off.

The sheriff was the first to spot Tyler and he immediately made a shushing sound and put his finger over his mouth as Kathleen, Jessie and Preston all spotted Tyler and their eyes went wide but they refrained from making a sound.

"We can't make any commotion," the sheriff insisted in a whispering tone. "The house is being watched."

"Should we turn off the lights?" Kathleen asked.

"They know we're here," the sheriff responded. "We just don't want to make any commotion to tip them off that Tyler is, too."

"Can I hug him?"

"Of course. Just do it behind a wall."

Tyler stepped back into the kitchen as his mom and his friends all followed him in and gave him a big group hug.

"Are you okay?" Jessie finally asked quietly.

"I'm fine," Tyler assured them all. "Where have you guys been?"

"Looking for you," Preston told him. "Had a small search party until about midnight. Then the sheriff sent his deputies home and the four of us drove around all night."

"How long have you been back here?" the sheriff asked.

"Just a couple of minutes."

"Where were you before that?" Kathleen asked him.

"I was hiding," Tyler confessed. "But, I'm done. At least for now."

"What does that mean, brah?" Preston was the first to ask.

"I saw the woman, Mom."

"Woah," Preston jumped in. "There's a woman? Is she hot?"

"No," Tyler said as he shook his head. "It's a long story. The point is, she knows all about this. She knew long before we did."

"She's your oracle," Preston said as if he was in the know.

"Something like that. Anyway, she told me not to hide. I think I can fulfill my destiny if I buy myself…"

"There's a destiny now?" Jessie asked, nervously.

"It would appear so," Tyler admitted with a bit of sadness. "I can do it if I buy myself a few days. I can only think of one way to do that."

"I'm listening," Kathleen told Tyler in an attempt to invite more information.

"McClean said he'll let me take my finals and graduate if I can make a deal with the feds."

"What kind of a deal?" Kathleen snapped.

"What are you going to do, turn yourself in?" the sheriff added.

"I'd get to graduate first."

"I don't care about that," Kathleen insisted. "You're not turning yourself in."

"You're right. I'm not."

"You're losing me," Kathleen said.

"Yeah," Preston added. "I think that one stumped us all."

"We'll strike a deal saying that I turn myself in after graduation. In the meantime, no agents and no press are allowed to hassle me."

"And if you're not turning yourself in, what happens after that?" Preston asked.

"They'll be waiting for you when it's over," the sheriff stated ardently. "They'll have the place surrounded."

"Let 'em," Tyler said with confidence.

"It's pretty risky," Kathleen shot back with a heavy dose of trepidation.

"What risk?" Tyler posed. "They know as well as I do they can't arrest me unless I let them. They'd have to kill me and I don't think they want to do that. This way they think they're getting me alive."

"So," Jessie started to ask, fearing she already knew the answer, "what do you do after graduation?"

"Destiny or no destiny, I disappear."

CHAPTER FORTY-FIVE
Graduation

The sheriff negotiated a deal with the Federal Bureau of Investigation that very same day. They balked at first but the sheriff quickly made them realize that the request was purely a courtesy. They really didn't have any choice in the matter. So, over the days that followed, Tyler was mostly left alone to live his life. He was constantly being stalked, but not pestered. It was very similar to life right before the incident with Graham and the fork outside of the cafeteria. Life in a fishbowl is better than life in a prison or a lab, at least for the prisoner or the rat.

Tyler was not allowed to attend his classes like he normally would have because the school was afraid of being litigated by Graham's parents or any other set of parents that might fear for the lives of their children. However, he was able to take his final exams in the privacy of Principal McClean's office and he, of course, aced them all.

Kathleen, Sheriff Wilson, Jessie, Preston, and Tyler were all in a constant state of anticipation as those days passed. No one knew when or where Tyler's big event would happen or what it would be, but they all expected something to happen sooner rather than later. There were a lot of emotional moments that took place as they all lived in fear that Tyler could be taken away at any moment. But, he used the time he had wisely and fulfilled his deepest wishes in order to make sure that if and when he went, there would be no regrets to leave behind.

Tyler was able to tell Preston that he forgave him and that he was the best friend a guy could ever hope to have. He was able to tell Jessie that he loved her and always had. He also insisted that she not say it back to him at that moment. He knew that she hadn't had as much time as he'd had to process everything and he didn't want her to say it until she was really sure. Of course, that came with a great deal of risk. Tyler could only hope that he would somehow be fortunate enough to be there when the time came.

He was able to thank the sheriff for all of his help and tell him that he hoped things worked out with his mom because he thought they were great together. And, last but certainly not least, he was able to tell his mom that in his mind, she was the true gift. His romantic love was clearly meant for Jessie. But, as is true for any boy with a healthy relationship with his mom, she would always remain his first love.

Finally, the days and nights leading up to it had all passed and graduation day arrived for the 1997 senior class of Penuel High School. The old gym was small and packed with spectators, including Kathleen and the sheriff who were sitting together. The graduating class of a little over one hundred students was seated in folding chairs on the basketball court, listening to Principal McClean introduce Jessie as the valedictorian speaker.

When he was finished, Jessie nervously stood to loud applause. Tyler and Preston may very well have been the loudest in the bunch as she climbed the stairs to the stage and approached the podium.

Tyler couldn't help but be surprised that he had made it to this moment. A bit of doubt had crept in and he wondered if he would actually have to go into hiding and possibly miss his miracle. He had planned to make a run for it immediately following the graduation while the crowds of students and proud family members made the scene chaotic enough to cause distractions. The sheriff had agreed to pick him up at the same campground where he had hid the last time. From there, he was simply trusting the sheriff who said he had everything worked out.

"Graduation is both a time to look forward and a time to look back," Jessie started. "It is a time to face our ambitions, our fears, and our regrets."

Graham was glaring at Tyler. When Tyler spotted this, he simply shook his head and looked away to let Graham know he wasn't afraid of him and thought of him as little more than a childish gorilla.

"It is a time to thank those who helped you make it through those tough, sometimes lonely years," Jessie continued. "We thank our parents, our teachers, our siblings, our coaches, and our friends."

Tyler looked over at Preston and smiled as Jessie took a minute to gather her thoughts. The trio's friendship had finally healed. Jessie realized in that minute that the speech she originally planned simply didn't make sense any longer. She folded the notes she had in front of her and stared out at the crowd.

"I know you're expecting me to make some attempt at being eloquent and profound today," she started back in as her gaze scanned the many faces of her fellow students. "But, I'm going to be real with you instead. As your valedictorian, I learned everything I could from teachers and books in my four years here. But, in the last week or so, I've learned far more from my friends."

Tyler looked up into the crowd of loved ones. He found his mom and the sheriff sitting together. Everything felt good and right in that moment. He glanced above their heads and spotted, just a few rows behind them, the elderly woman who had appeared to him at the campground. He was so happy until that moment that the sighting took a second or two to register in his brain. His heart rate suddenly increased as panic set in.

"I would like to take this opportunity to thank one of those friends in particular," Jessie continued. "He's on everyone's mind right now so, this seems especially fitting. I've known Tyler Hirsch my whole life. I've loved him my whole life. Even when I was embarrassed to show it."

The sound of his name caught Tyler's attention. He looked back up at Jessie but his mind was still on that woman until he heard Jessie say she loved him. That statement was a welcome distraction from the inevitable and copious distress that came with seeing the elderly woman sitting in the bleachers.

"I don't care what anyone else thinks of him," Jessie said with a warm smile on her face, "whether you're scared of him or whatever, Tyler Hirsch is a true friend…not just to me or Preston, but to all of us." She wiped the tears that she couldn't help from falling off of her face as she continued to speak. "He has been to me my whole life. Even when I didn't return the favor. But, it even goes beyond that. The love I have for Tyler is the deepest thing I've ever felt outside of my relationship with God. It has always been there, even when I suppressed it, and it's something that won't go away no matter what happens next."

The crowd began to mumble as people reacted to Jessie's words. She and Tyler looked directly into each other's eyes. Both were overcome with tears. As they wiped their faces in failed attempts to keep their cheeks dry, Tyler glanced back up in the bleachers just in time to see the elderly woman stand.

Suddenly, the entire building began to shake, slow at first, but escalating rapidly. Tyler looked back at Jessie who had instantly become terrified. His eyes then floated up into the bleachers again but the elderly woman was no longer there. He looked at the sheriff and his mom, then over to Preston, and finally back to Jessie as they all quickly realized that his time had come.

CHAPTER FORTY-SIX
A Date With Destiny

The people in the stands looked around, first thinking that someone might be stomping on the bleachers. They quickly realized, however, that the stage and podium were shaking as well. Soon, even the walls seemed to be moving. And then, it became abundantly clear that nothing at all was stationary.

Preston looked over at Tyler, who was just as confused as everyone else, and then up at Jessie who was already fixated on Tyler as if he could offer some kind of answer. Tyler looked at each of them, almost apologizing for not knowing more than anyone else. All he could think of was what each of them already knew, which was that this must be the big event. Under the circumstances, that knowledge seemed completely worthless. He didn't know what it was or what he was supposed to do about it.

The shaking quickly grew fierce and the scoreboard crashed to the ground. The glass backboards on the basketball court began to shatter and walls started to crack. The thunderous rumbling sounds were terrifying.

"Earthquake!" a man shouted as he bounded to his feet in horror.

The people in the stands began to flee, trampling each other on their way to the exits. The sound of the rumbling below was nearly overpowered by the screams of the frightened mob.

"Everyone stay calm!" the sheriff shouted, trying to steady the chaos. "Stay calm!" Sheriff Wilson quickly realized that his effort was futile. No one had any sort of peace or calm and he couldn't blame them. Instead, he started to help people who were being knocked down by frantic passers by to get back up on their feet. "Kathleen, get out of here. This old building won't hold for long."

"What about you?" she inquired out of sincere concern for his well-being. "What about the kids?"

"Everyone needs to get out, now!" he asserted.

The basketball court was starting to ripple. People were falling down, both from the vibrations and from the force of other people. Boards were popping out of the floor and chairs were bouncing all over the room.

A large piece of the ceiling began to fall on the center of the court, threatening the lives of at least a dozen students. Tyler spotted it and telekinetically smashed it into millions of harmless pieces.

Cracks continued to spread up the walls and out over the ceiling. It was clear that the old building would soon cave in and kill everyone who was left inside.

As people continued to fearfully lose self-control and trample each other, Tyler looked around the room with a peculiar sense of calmness. He knew that he could somehow save these people from certain death. This was his purpose. He was answering the call.

Standing in the middle of the rippling basketball court with frantic people running all around him, Tyler raised his arms and pushed back against the gravitational pull just in time to keep the roof and walls from caving in.

"Get out of here, Preston," Tyler insisted. Preston stood up, otherwise motionless. "You want to help?" Tyler asked. "Get out and take Jessie with you."

Preston spun around and saw Jessie moving toward them as quickly as she could. He rushed to help her.

Passing through the exit, Graham looked back and spotted Tyler holding the walls together. For the first time, his heart warmed toward Tyler and he actually felt grateful. Guilt would soon set in but, at this moment, he only had enough time to flee for safety.

With the sheriff chasing her, Kathleen fought the crowd and

finally reached her son. "Tyler, what are you doing?" she shouted.

"Holding it back," Tyler said peacefully.

"Tyler, we have to get out of here," Kathleen contended.

The sheriff finally caught up to Kathleen as Tyler answered her. "You have to get out of here," he told her. "You all do. If I let go, everyone in here dies."

There were so many cracks in the walls and ceiling, they looked like shattered glass. People fought their way through the exits and the room finally started to empty.

"If you don't let go," the sheriff told Tyler, "you'll die."

Everyone left in the room could barely stand up against the ripple of the floor beneath them.

"This is it," Tyler said with an almost eerie calm. "This is the moment I was made for. They need to know miracles still happen."

"Who needs to know," Kathleen asked as tears streamed down her face like someone had opened a valve.

"Everyone."

All five of them were given the time to prepare for this moment. Still, Tyler was the only one truly ready to accept it.

"This can't be it!" Kathleen shouted.

"There's no more time. Get out!" Tyler finally shouted as he realized he was growing weaker.

"Tyler," Jessie yelled as she and Preston approached from

behind him. "Please!"

"Sheriff?!" Tyler insisted.

The sheriff looked around at the now nearly empty, but destroyed, gymnasium. He took Kathleen by the arm and Preston followed his lead by doing the same with Jessie. Kathleen and Jessie became hysterical as Sheriff Wilson and Preston dragged them away.

"Get them out there," the sheriff shouted to Preston as they reached the exit.

"What about you?" Kathleen screamed at the sheriff through her sobbing. "I can't lose you both!"

"Go!" the sheriff shouted back as Preston held the girls and tried to drag them both outside. As the door closed, Sheriff Wilson walked briskly toward Tyler.

"Get out of here, Sheriff," Tyler said as he dropped to his knees in exhaustion. "I'm serious. I can't hold it back much longer."

"You're coming with me," the sheriff persisted.

Several ceiling pieces fell as the earthquake finally subsided.

"Aaaarrrrggggghhh!" Tyler shouted in pain. The endurance of his powers was being tested and they had about reached their limits.

"I don't know how," the sheriff yelled, "but somehow, you're coming with me!"

"When I let go," Tyler said through heavy breaths, "this building's coming down. It's just not possible!"

"Listen," the sheriff asserted as if he'd found the answer he was looking for. "It's over."

"This thing is still coming down," Tyler maintained.

"I can't let you…"

"Sheriff," Tyler interrupted in a hurry, "if you don't get out of here, you're going to die, too! My mom needs you now more than she ever has before!"

Tyler was right and putting Kathleen into the equation finally made the sheriff see it clearly. In that moment, Sheriff Wilson made the hardest decision of his entire life. With a nod of understanding and appreciation, he started backing up toward the exit. He finally turned and jogged to the doors. He opened them up and took one last look just in time to see Tyler collapse in exhaustion.

The sheriff dove out of the building and rolled to safety as it imploded all around Tyler. The walls and ceiling completely caved in. The floor gave way and fell into the foundation. Debris and dust clouds went everywhere as the crackling boom sounds pierced the air and could be heard for miles.

When it was over, lying buried deep beneath the rubble, was Tyler's lifeless body.

CHAPTER FORTY-SEVEN
Birthday Funeral

Grief is, perhaps, the most intolerable emotion that a human being can feel. It is a deep, anguishing heartache that always brings sorrow and pain. Grief can also produce regret, guilt and even shame. Most would agree that it is the definitive form of unhappiness.

All of these emotions and so many more were felt at Tyler Hirsch's funeral. Some of the emotions may have seemed out of place at a funeral, especially the funeral of a teenager. They even included a few that were actually the direct opposite of the ones stemming from grief, like wonder, gladness, and even joy. These emotions and so many more were all amplified by the fact that this funeral was being held on what otherwise would have been Tyler's eighteenth birthday.

It was the biggest service the town had ever experienced. From townspeople who actually knew him, to the local, state, national and even some international media, everyone seemed to be there. Non-media people who had never heard the name Tyler Hirsch until the weeks that preceded it drove in from Seattle, Washington, McMinville, Oregon, Billings, Montana and even as far away as Albuquerque, New

Mexico to pay their respects to the young man who had performed this miracle that had saved so many lives.

The service was broadcast live on national television, and even picked up in some international markets, as if a famous world leader had passed away. Even the Pope watched from Vatican City. There were rumors that Tyler would be made a saint but most dismissed that rumor because Tyler wasn't part of a local, Catholic church in front of which testimonies could be presented to deem him Venerable. Only time would tell whether or not the church found a way around that obstacle.

At the service, Jessie stood with Preston, sobbing. She felt profound loss, of course. But, she also felt regret over the time she had wasted, trying to be the popular girl in school, that could have been spent with someone who loved her for who she truly was. Now, that person was gone forever. Her only comfort was the short time they had together before his death and the fact that she had found the courage to confess her love for him with no time to spare.

Preston had regrets of his own, but they were more recent than Jessie's. While Jessie had the wonderful memories with Preston and Tyler from her childhood, Preston had the joy of continuing those memories right up until the earthquake took the life of his best friend, five days prior to this moment. He was thankful that Tyler had forgiven him for his mistakes so that they would not be the final memories they shared. Instead, his final memories were those of attempting to help Tyler and then watching the heroic actions Tyler performed in his last breaths.

Kathleen was nearly cried out by the time the funeral had started. As the sheriff held her tightly, a few tears still spilled out. But the three days after the quake had been the hardest for her. She rode the rollercoaster of hope and despair while digging through the rubble and searching for Tyler's body went on and on for what felt like weeks. The tear flow peaked when Tyler was found dead. It was so final. That was the moment that nearly dried out her tear ducts.

Principal McClean and his wife stood with other faculty members like Mr. Brooks, Mr. Russell and the custodian, Dan Bailey. They would miss the wonderful student that had roamed the hallways and sat in their classes, but the burden of their sorrows would fade more quickly than those of Tyler's mom and close friends.

Even Graham Zimmerman showed up feeling remorseful about how hard he'd been on Tyler. But, far more shocking than Graham's attendance was the fact that even Brett Riggle showed up. However, he had gained so much weight he was forced to walk with a cane and he had grown a beard that would make ZZ Top jealous. So, no one recognized him and he didn't have the courage to approach Kathleen. She never knew he was there. Brett Riggle was simply there to pay respects to the son he never knew. Talk about a man with regrets.

Also in attendance, of course, were all of the people Tyler had healed before his death. The people who had been knocking on death's door in the hospital's intensive care unit and Nancy Hanley, all felt sorry to see Tyler go, but also such gratefulness for the lives he had given back to them before he went.

There was a collective sense of pride from the people of Penuel and the surrounding towns. In the same way everyone who lived near Seattle when the grunge sound was popular in music claimed Seattle as home, the number of people claiming Penuel suddenly skyrocketed. They felt blessed that this miracle had happened in their midst. That it was a son of this geographical area who had been used in such a magnificent way. And, the more people knew Tyler, the more pride was felt.

Most of the eyes in attendance filled with tears as the preacher from Penuel Community Church talked about Tyler as a gift from God. He mentioned seeing Tyler and Kathleen in the congregation over the years. The truth was, they had attended many times but Kathleen knew they weren't as consistent as she would have liked and that had become a regret. The preacher declared that Tyler had been sent to the world, and Penuel in particular, as a demonstration of God's gracious love. He read the first few verses of Psalm 46, which says "God is our refuge and strength, an ever-present help in trouble. Therefore we will not fear, though the earth give way and the mountains fall into the heart of the sea, though its waters roar and foam and the mountains quake with their surging." He declared Tyler and the people who performed the miracles in Japan, Chile and Finland, the greatest reminders of the fact that God is our refuge since He, in the ultimate act of love, sent his one and only Son to keep all who believe in Him from perishing and, instead, grant them eternal life.

As the preacher announced that he would be performing baptisms in the Yakima River following the service, a TV reporter, who stood at the edge of the cemetery grounds, quietly re-capped the news story to her audience. She revealed some of the scientific mystery surrounding Tyler's event that demonstrated the impact beyond Penuel.

"Five days after the devastating earthquake," the reporter described, "with an epicenter right here in Penuel, the entire town has gathered to mourn the loss of its only victim. Seventeen year-old Tyler Hirsch, who would have turned eighteen today but whose body was found two days ago, is said to have saved the lives of more than a thousand townspeople in what is being called a modern day miracle. While a thousand people in and around a small town high school gymnasium might not sound as significant as recent comparable events in Tokyo, Santiago, or Helsinki, where the estimated number of lives saved can reach six figures, the miracle here in Penuel might be even more monumental than it first appeared. Seismologists are having trouble measuring the earthquake, stating that the amount of energy released does not even come close to matching the impact of the elastic waves. Could this have something to do with the miracle of Tyler Hirsch? Did he save the lives of countless others in towns all over Eastern Washington? While witnesses say he was holding back the walls of the building that they were in, could he also have been holding back the very earth itself?"

CHAPTER FORTY-EIGHT
Impending

Several months after the funeral, Jessie found herself sitting in the shaded grass under a large tree on a one hundred and eight acre college campus in Newberg, Oregon. She had attended her first two classes and was starting to read one of her textbooks when footsteps approached from behind her and a pair of hands suddenly covered her eyes, startling her.

"Guess who?" suggested a voice she didn't immediately recognize due to the person's over-the-top disguise attempt that made him sound like a bad Fat Albert impersonator.

"Well, since this is my first day of classes and I don't really know anyone here…" she retorted, nervously. "This is more than a little bit creepy.

"Close your eyes," the stranger exclaimed.

"Why?" Jessie asked, skeptically.

"Just play along."

"It's against my better judgment but fine," Jessie reluctantly agreed.

Slowly but surely, Jessie felt the hands release from her face and heard the footsteps of the person as he walked around and knelt in front of her.

"Okay," the person said, quietly. "Open 'em."

Jessie slowly opened her eyes and her mouth gradually followed as shock and confusion washed over her. Her body began to shake and her eyes filled with tears. "Are you really there?" she asked, barely able to get the words out as she stared Tyler directly in the face.

He looked different. His hair was darker, he was wearing glasses that she assumed were fake, and he'd changed his style to look a little more hip. "Yeah," Tyler said with a massive grin. "It's me."

Jessie went to hug him but he held up a hand to stop her. "Not out here," he warned her. "No one can know we knew each other before this."

"What do you mean?" she inquired out of confusion.

"I mean," Tyler started in while extending a hand to shake, "I'm Jake."

"Jake?" she asked, still confused.

"That's right."

"Okay," she said as she took his hand and shook it, beginning to play along. "I'm Jessie."

"Nice to meet you, Jessie."

"You, too," Jessie said, having to fight even harder against the tears. She was unable to release his hand because the touch made the moment real. She slowly allowed herself to believe more and more and couldn't bear the thought of ever letting go again. "Now, do you mind telling me why I didn't come out of my room for a week after my friend Tyler's funeral? And why, regardless of his name and weird hair and clothes, he's currently right here in front of me?"

Tyler finally sat down in front of her and inhaled deeply as they continued to hold each other's hand. "I was gone for a couple of days," he began to tell her as he exhaled.

"A couple of days?" she interrupted. "It's been months, Tyler."

"I mean gone-gone."

"As in dead gone?"

"I'm not even sure how to describe it," he explained as he thought back on his experience. "But, I learned so much. There's so much to tell you."

"My next class isn't for another hour and a half," she told him, insisting he spill it now.

"This'll take a lot longer than that."

"So, get started."

"I showed up out in the middle of nowhere," Tyler told her. "At least twenty miles from town. I was hungry. I was thirsty. My body hadn't been touched the whole time. Like the earth had swallowed me up and then finally spit me back out again. My body was dead during those three days but my spirit was conscious and that's how I learned about what was coming."

"What's coming?" Jessie asked, eagerly.

"I didn't reach civilization until two o'clock in the morning," Tyler continued, skipping over Jessie's question for now. "But, as soon as I did, I called Sheriff Wilson collect from a pay-phone and his guy in the C.I.A. took care of everything from there."

"What about the casket?" Jessie inquired, wiping her tears away. "What about your body being found in the first place?"

"The sheriff's guy took care of all of it in a matter of hours," Tyler told her. "It was incredible. The corpse they pulled out of the rubble was totally staged. I don't know how he pulled it off so fast but it was someone else's body they planted there and the casket was full of sandbags. I'm sorry I couldn't tell you. They wouldn't let me. My mom didn't even know until two days after the funeral. It had to look real, you know?"

"I get it," she said as Tyler reached forward and wiped more tears from her face. "I heard Sheriff Wilson got a job in Seattle and your mom went with him."

"They're actually in San Diego. Doug and Judy Nelson."

"Really?"

"Yep. That's where I'm from now, too. I'm a transfer student from San Diego State. I've already got a year of college under my belt. Something of an athlete, too."

"Just the kind of guy I've been hoping to meet at college," Jessie said with a smile.

"And here I am."

"And here you are," she said. As her smile brightened, a tear raced down her left cheek. "Amazing."

There was a brief pause in the conversation in which Jessie and Tyler silently shared both the joy of being back together and the weight of what they had been through.

"You know," Jessie finally started back in, "you could have picked a better name than Jake."

"What's wrong with Jake?"

"Nothing. Not by itself. But, we're obviously going to be a couple now."

"Slow your roll, little lady. Jake and Jessie just met."

After a playful exchange of smiles, "Jake and Jessie. Two 'J' names. That's not corny to you?"

"I was going more for cute," Tyler admitted a bit sheepishly. "But, then I heard it when I said it out loud for the first time and, maybe I didn't think that all the way through."

"No turning back now," Jessie said with a smile.

"Nope."

"I'll take it," she said, unable to wipe the permanent smile off her face. There was another pause as the two of them just enjoyed being in each other's presence. Finally, Jessie started again. "Whatever it was that was happening in the world ended with you. Japan, Chile, Finland, you, then nothing."

"Actually," Tyler corrected her, "that was just the beginning. A warning sign of what's coming."

"There you go again," Jessie pointed out, referring to the fact that he left her hanging on a similar declaration once before. "What's coming?"

"A war," Tyler said very seriously. "A spiritual war that has been going on for thousands of years for the souls of all mankind. A war that has only been fought on a plane humans couldn't see. But, that's changing. The final battle will be fought, very soon, right here. For all to see."

Tyler let that sink in for a moment and Jessie stared back at him. If somebody had made a statement like that to her four or five months ago, she would have blown them off as a total nut-job. Now, and from Tyler, she knew it was true.

"Those couple of days might as well have been centuries," Tyler finally continued. "The spiritual world isn't bound by time the way the physical world is. We were…"

"We?" Jessie interrupted for clarification.

"The four of us. We were gathering armies."

"Four of you, as in the other miracles?" she asked, needing additional clarification.

"Exactly," Tyler explained. We were each given an element. Rio comes from the East. She controls the waters. Matias comes from the South. He controls fire. Amanda comes from the North. She controls the winds. Then there's me. I control the earth."

"So, you still have your powers?" Jessie said with a grin. "You can still do all of those things?"

Tyler's smile widened. "And a whole lot more."

THE GIFT OF TYLER

THE GIFT OF THE ELEMENTS SERIES
BY C.S. ELSTON

Also by C.S. Elston

Now Available:

"The Four Corners"

"The Gift of Rio"

"The Four Corners of Darkness"

Coming Soon:

"The Four Corners of Winter"

"The Gift of Matias"

"The Gift of Amanda"

After award-winning stage work in the nineties, Chris Elston moved to Los Angeles where he wrote more than two dozen feature film and television screenplays. He has been invited to participate in screenwriting events for Cinema Seattle and Angel Citi Film Festival. In 2013, Chris left Los Angeles for the suburbs of his hometown, Seattle, Washington, to get married and start a new chapter in his own story. Five and a half years later, the journey of the chapter that followed landed he and his wife in Prescott, Arizona where they now reside.

You can learn more at:
cselston.com
twitter.com/cselston
facebook.com/cselston